COVER
DISSECT DESIGNS
WWW.DISSECTDESIGNS.COM

Copyright © 2019 Stephen Taylor

All rights reserved.

ISBN: 9798549161849

DANNY PEARSON WILL RETURN

For updates about current and upcoming releases, as well as exclusive promotions, visit the authors website at:

www.stephentaylorbooks.com

Vodka Over London Ice

Stephen Taylor

ONE

Under a cloud-covered night sky, four figures exited a Russian-built Mi-8 helicopter into the dry Afghanistan wasteland. They fanned out, taking a knee, rifles up at the ready. Their eyes scanned the terrain through night scopes. The helicopter's engines grew louder, the increased downdraft peppering their backs with stinging grit as it left. As soon as the noise died away, the team leader signalled them onwards. It had dropped them five miles from their target destination to avoid detection. They broke into a fast tab to cover the distance. Checking his GPS, the lead signalled stop. They drank to rehydrate as streams of sweat ran down their grease-painted faces. The SAS team lay on their bellies, peeping over the ridge of a dried-up riverbed. Smudge focused through his night sight, keeping watch through the eerie green enhanced view on their target. The team's leader,

Danny Pearson, ran through the intel and mission plan one last time.

'Ok, guys, intel puts the hostages in this compound here. Our objective is to get diplomat Richard Mann, his wife and his son out. If we can do that without things turning into a shitstorm, all the better,' said Danny, tapping the aerial reconnaissance photo.

'We'll follow the natural cover of the riverbed to here. On the all clear, we'll have to sprint the final forty metres of open ground up to the wall. Ok?' He paused for the teams' affirmation.

'At the wall, Smudge, Chaz, you cover the alley to the north and our exit route south. Me and Fergus will enter the compound here and extract the hostages.'

Their senses heightened as the rising adrenaline flowed through their veins.

'Remember, if the shit hits the fan, lay down heavy covering fire and get back here. I'll call in an air strike and we'll move out for extraction. Ok?'

Following the plan, they moved along the low-lying riverbed. It wound left and right until it eventually cornered close to the wall. Heads barely over the bank, they checked out the compound through their sights.

'Guard two o'clock, top of the east corner,' said Chaz.

'Roger that,' said Danny.

'Guard heading away from us up the northern alley,' said Smudge, scanning the far corner.

'I see him. Roger that.'

They watched for a few more minutes to be sure no more guards were on sentry duty. The drone images in their mission intel showed around a dozen Al Qaeda fighters in the compound.

'Guard on the wall is moving away,' said Chaz, his eyes still glued to the target.

'Ok, get set, we move on three.'

Danny paused for a few more seconds to make sure the guard didn't turn back.

'One, two, three.'

Moving as fast as they could with forty kilos of kit on their backs, the men ran tight and low to the base of the compound wall. Swivelling around they planted their backs against it, guns immediately up as the four of them covered every direction, listening.

Silence. No yelling, no alarm raised.

'Right, let's get this done by the book, guys. No heroics,' said Danny, waving off Smudge and Chaz to cover the far corner while he and Fergus headed for the compound entrance.

Two metres from the corner, Smudge lay down on his front while Chaz took a knee, his back to Smudge as he covered the rear and Danny's exit route. Moving incredibly slowly Smudge edged forward in silence in the dark. He got his eyes around the corner and looked up the northern alley. His eyes searched in the one dim light source from a lamp at the top of the alley. To his surprise a red dot appeared no more than four metres away. A guard's face glowed red as he leaned back against the wall and sucked on his cigarette.

Fighting the urge to flinch away, Smudge inched back behind the corner. He tapped Chaz on the shoulder and signalled eyes on one. Sliding off his pack and rifle he pulled his knife and turned back. Chaz stood glued to the corner, silenced gun at the ready if needed. Smudge moved painstakingly slowly into the darkness of the alley.

Bored and tired, the guard finished his cigarette, throwing the butt to the ground. He reached for his rifle propped up against the wall. He didn't get close. A hand clamped over his mouth, the feeling of cold steel against his hot neck barely having time to register. Smudge thrust the knife up into the base of his skull, killing him instantly.

'Contact. Hostile down. Mission still a go,' came over Danny's earpiece.

'Roger that. Entering compound now.'

Keeping as flat against the wall as he could, Danny crouched by the arched entrance to the compound. Reaching into his pack, he removed a little telescopic rod with a mirror attached. Extending it slowly at floor level, he twisted it around until he finally picked up the reflection of two guards just inside.

'Two. Ten yards in, right-hand side,' he whispered into his throat mic.

'Roger that,' came Fergus's whispered reply.

'I'll take those two, you cover my back and look for the one up on the wall,' whispered Danny, packing the mirror stick away and exchanging it for his suppressed rifle.

'Roger that,' came Fergus's reply, as he tucked in tighter behind Danny.

'On my mark. You all clear, Smudge?'

Lying on top of the dead guard as he covered the alley, Smudge nodded to Chaz.

'Affirmative, good to go.'

Danny swung around through the arch, eyeing the guards. He double-tapped two shots into centre mass of each guard, dropping them like a stone. Another couple of metallic pings sounded behind him, followed by a thud as the guard fell off the wall onto the dirt floor. They took a knee with guns up, covering the courtyard in anticipation of attack. No alarm. No guards. All quiet.

The two of them dragged the bodies behind a beaten-up old pickup truck parked against the compound wall. They continued towards the building that on the satellite pictures was marked as the hostage location.

'Hostiles down. Proceeding to hostage location,' whispered Danny over the mic.

'Roger that. Perimeter clear,' replied Chaz.

They moved low past the first building. Lights were on and they could hear voices chattering and laughing through the open windows. Danny moved in the lead to the door of the hostage block, with Fergus walking backwards, covering the rear.

'I'll take point, you take my left,' whispered Danny as they both stood, ready to storm the building.

'Roger that.'

Moving through the door fast, they fell into a well-practiced search manoeuvre. As they swept through the rooms, they found no guards. The reason became clear as soon as they entered the last room. Lying on the ground three feet away from his own head, was the diplomat's decapitated body. Lying next to him on their sides with their hands tied behind them lay his wife and son with their throats cut, their faces locked in the terrifying last moments of life.

They stood locked, unable to pull away from the scene for a few long seconds. The smell of death and sound of buzzing flies was etching its way into their memories forever.

'Fuck! Fucking bastards,' said Danny, the shock sending his mind spiralling. His own wife and child had been killed a couple of years ago, when a lorry driver crushed their car before driving off, never to be found. Deep suppressed feelings came flooding to the surface as he looked at the bodies in front of him, images of his wife and son appearing over the top of them as his mind overloaded with emotion.

'Fucking bastards. Bastards.'

'Mission abort. Hostages are dead. We're coming out. Prepare for evac,' said Fergus, tapping Danny on the shoulder.

'Roger that,' came Smudge's reply.

'Danny—time to go, mate.'

Dazed, Danny followed Fergus out the door without responding. As they passed the building with the lights on Danny stopped.

'Fucking bastards,' he kept muttering over and over.

'Danny! What you doin', Boss?' asked Fergus, watching horrified as Danny charged the door. Inside the shocked Al Qaeda fighters stumbled and tripped out of their chairs, trying frantically to grab their rifles. A hail of fully automatic fire ripped through the room. Blood and plaster filled the air. None of them managed to get a round off before Danny's gun clicked empty. As the dust settled, the door from the kitchen burst open and a screaming fanatic hurtled towards him with a meat cleaver in his hand. Still enraged beyond reason, Danny dropped his rifle and charged directly at the man, pulling his commando knife from its sheath as he went. A second before contact, the man flew backwards onto a bunk in a cloud of red mist, three rounds from Fergus's rifle hitting him squarely in the chest.

Danny pulled to a stop, breathing heavily with a tear rolling down his cheek. Fergus came up next to him and put his arm around his shoulder.

'Come on, mate, it's over. Let's go home.'

His face hard as granite, Danny wiped his eyes, turned and picked up his rifle. Loading a fresh magazine into it, he walked out of the building.

'Smudge, Chaz, we're coming out. Clear for evac,' he said.

'All clear, Boss, come on out.'

I can't do this anymore—I'm done.

TWO

Harry Knight sat on a kitchen stool, reading his morning paper over the white marble-topped breakfast bar. His wife, Louise, clicked around the kitchen in her high heels. He dressed immaculately as always; this morning's choice a Saville Row charcoal suit and matching waistcoat, snuggly fitted over a crisp white shirt and dark grey silk tie. His platinum submariner Rolex was just visible under shirt cuffs held together with diamond-encrusted gold HK cufflinks.

'Thanks, love,' he said as his wife put a cup on a coaster in front of him.

'Right, I'm off now, Harry. I've got to drop May off at college then I'm meeting the girls for lunch later,' said Louise, kissing him on the cheek as she grabbed her Gucci handbag and keys.

'Ok, love. I've gotta go to the club tonight so I'll be late home,' he shouted after her. He heard an 'Ok' echo back from the hall, followed by her calling for their daughter. May's face appeared around the door to the lounge, a carefree, happy smile spread widely across it.

'Bye, Dad,' she said.

'Bye, darlin'. Have a good day,' he said softly back.

'Coming!' she shouted, disappearing out the other door.

Harry could hear Louise talking to someone at the front door.

'Harry, Bob's here. Go through, love. He's in the kitchen,' she said, slamming the front door in her hurry to leave.

Bob Angel came in through the kitchen door at an angle; the size of his shoulders wouldn't fit head-on. The ex-bare knuckle fighter was sporting a little middle-age spread these days, but that aside, he still cast a formidable shadow. He was dressed in a dark blue tailored suit. It looked out of place for a man with a flat crooked nose and hands like shovels but Harry insisted all his guys wore smart suits.

'We're businessmen, not street thugs,' he'd say.

'All right, Bob, what brings you here this early? You were at the club til four, weren't you?' said Harry, looking up from his paper. 'You wanna coffee?'

Harry got up and moved around the kitchen to make his oldest friend and right-hand man a drink.

'Yes, please, Boss. I'm round early cause we've had a bit of trouble at the club and down the Dog-n-Duck,' said Bob, the stool creaking under his weight.

Frowning, Harry put the drink down on a coaster in front of Bob. He picked up his own and remained standing.

'Go on,' he said.

'We caught one of Volkov's guys dealing in the club again last night, and Pete's had two of them approach him in the Dog. They threatened him, said he had to use them to supply the booze to the pub, or else,' said Bob, his thick cockney accent remaining calm.

'Viktor fucking Volkov, that cheeky Russian bastard,' said Harry, turning his back to Bob. He looked out the large bi-folding patio doors, thinking. A workman was jet-washing his patio while the gardener inspected his carefully manicured lawn.

'That little prick's been warned about this before and he's still takin' the piss. Get some of the lads together, track down Viktor's scummy little runners and give them a good hidin'—not enough to put 'em in hospital, but hard enough that they don't forget it. Tell them to fuck off back south of the river and stay there,' he said, turning back to Bob and spilling his coffee on the breakfast bar as he put it down.

'Shit, better mop that up. Lou will have my guts for garters.'

Bob chuckled to himself. The great Harry Knight— the man who built an empire of pubs, clubs, betting shops and property any way he could was still not the boss of his own home.

'How's the fight coming along, Bob?' asked Harry, getting back to business.

'Good, Harry, the kid looks mustard. Bets are well up. The other guy's a four-to-one long-shot. He's a good lad, happy with the bung. He'll go down in the third,' said Bob, beaming. He still loved the thrill of the fight game.

'Great. The warehouse all set up ok?' asked Harry, his mood lifting.

'Yeah, invitation only and Mark's sorted all the security - no phones, no filming. All set up like a charity event. We've even got some talent from local clubs doing boxing bouts. Once they're all done, we'll move 'em out before the bare knuckle bout,' said Bob, taking a gulp of his drink.

'What do the figures look like?'

Bob's big hands pulled a little notebook from his inside pocket. He thumbed through the curled-up edges before finding the page he wanted.

'We've got some big boys betting. Should clear seventy, maybe eighty grand.'

'Good work. Anything else I need to know about?' asked Harry, sliding his suit jacket off the back of the kitchen chair and moving towards the hall.

'No, Boss, we're all good,' said Bob, getting off the creaking chair and following him out the door.

Harry put his jacket on, spending the time to check his appearance in the mirror. He adjusted his collar and straightened his silk tie.

'Right. I've got an appointment with the planning office. Let's see if that greasy councillor's earned his money and got us planning permission. I'm gonna see Maureen up the hospital afterwards.'

Satisfied with his appearance Harry opened the front door.

'How's she and the boys doing?' asked Bob, filling the door on his way out.

'Not good I'm afraid. The cancer's spread. They reckon it'll be weeks rather than months. Robert seems to be holding it together ok. We don't know about Danny; he's still in the Middle East somewhere. It'll hit him hard. It's only been a couple of years since the accident,' said Harry, suddenly standing in sombre silence.

'Well, say hello to your sister and Rob from me anyway, Boss. Tell them I'll be thinking of them.'

'Thanks, Bob. Now fuck off and get some sleep. I'll see you tonight.'

Bob nodded and walked across the crunchy gravel to his black Range Rover. He opened the door. The car rocked as he got in. Harry turned towards two black-suited men standing on the drive between the three other cars. They were heavy broad-shouldered men with wide necks and flattened noses, hand-picked by Harry and Bob from amateur boxing clubs in their youth.

'Tom, bring the Bentley round. We're going uptown,' he said before turning to the other one.

'Phil, take the Merc up the Polskis and get it cleaned for me. It looks a disgrace.'

Both men got on with their boss's instruction: you didn't keep Harry Knight waiting. The white Bentley swung round and stopped in front of him. Tom hopped out and moved around to open the passenger door. Leaving the house, the white Bentley with the HK1 number plates turned left, driving through the affluent St John's Wood, heading for the heart of London and the City of Westminster council buildings.

THREE

Wiping a tear from her freshly blackened eye, Ana stared at her reflection in the mirror of the en-suite bathroom. Today was her seventeenth birthday, but no one knew or cared. Six months ago she'd answered an ad in a Romanian newspaper for work in England. Full of optimism she'd travelled from her tiny village to the Bucharest agency. Since then she'd been tricked, trafficked, beaten, drugged and raped. With her spirit broken, she'd accepted her place as a plaything for Viktor to use, abuse, or sell for sex.

'Ana, where are you? Get your arse back to bed, bitch.'

His voice made her shake despite the vodka and cocaine haze. She hurried back to the bedroom - one black eye was enough for now. Moving across the thick carpet, she climbed onto the super king-sized bed, its slippery white silk sheets cool to the touch. Viktor was kneeling over Selina. He sniffed lines of cocaine off her breasts with a fifty pound note. She wriggled and moaned in a well-rehearsed act of pleasure and excitement. Selina knew the game as well as Ana: play to survive. Ana tucked in close behind Viktor. She reached around him and went to work.

Ignoring his groans and grunts, she looked over his shoulder at the spectacular view from the penthouse. The glistening Thames cut London in half while a mixture of old and new buildings jostled for position on either side: The Shard, St Paul's Cathedral, the London Eye and Houses of Parliament. All the power and money, such an affluent country. Her heart sank. All she wanted to do was get away and run back to her family in the poor little village in Romania.

The phone ringing broke Viktor's concentration. He threw Ana off him to answer it.

'Shit,' he said, looking at the ID, rubbing and slapping his face to remove the fog in his head.

'Yuri, good to hear from you.'

'Viktor! How is my little brother? Are you making progress over there?' asked Yuri, his cold, confident voice floating down the phone.

'Da, everything is good, Brother. No need to concern yourself. The heroin and cocaine sells well here, and the fat businessmen pay top money for the girls. Tell Papa is good,' said Viktor, sniffing and rubbing the remnants of coke off his nose.

'Good, that is good. So your men didn't get thrown out of Harry Knight's club last night?' asked Yuri, dropping into silence at the end to rattle him.

Viktor's face dropped as he searched his foggy brain for a response.

Fucking Dimitri. He must have been talking to Dimitri.

'Is nothing, it's a small problem, Yuri. Tell Papa I'm on top of it,' said Viktor, doing his best to sound sober and calm.

'Papa has stepped down, Viktor. I'm in charge of the business now.'

'Congratulations, Brother. Is no need to worry. Everything here is good,' said Viktor through gritted teeth, his head spinning and mood darkening.

Fucking golden boy Yuri. Papa always gave him everything. Now I have to answer to the bastard.

Yuri's cold voice came back at him.

'I certainly hope so, little brother. I don't want to have to come over there.'

Viktor could picture his smug face revelling in his newly acquired power over him.

'Is no problem, Yuri. Is under control.'

Viktor ended the call without answering. He threw the phone across the room, the anger rising inside him as he rose from the bed.

'What are you staring at, whore?' he shouted towards Selina.

'Nothing, Viktor. Please, come back to bed,' she said, trying to pacify him. Ana put her arms around his shoulders, desperately trying to calm him. The anger and jealousy of his brother was building beyond containment and the two women were in the line of fire.

Without warning, he punched Ana to the floor, kicking her in the stomach repeatedly until she coughed and retched. Still furious he turned his attention to Selina as she backed away. He picked up a wide leather belt with a heavy metal buckle off the bedroom chair. With Ana still on the floor trying to get air in her lungs, he walked slowly towards the bed. Selina sat drawing her knees to her chest, the tears beginning to flow as she shook her head.

'No, Viktor, please no.'

FOUR

The corridor of the private hospital was decorated nicer than its NHS equivalent. Prints of famous water coloured paintings adorned the walls. Flowers sat in vases on choice bits of furniture placed in between the private room doors.

Dress it up anyway you like, there was no coming back from the terminally ill wing of a hospital.

Harry Knight stopped outside the door and stared at the little typed removable name tag. He pushed his thoughts down deep and sucked up a smile. He tapped lightly and entered.

Rob looked up from his seat beside his mum and beckoned Harry in. Maureen Pearson was asleep. Her skin was as pale as ivory and she looked painfully thin and frail and lost in the bed.

'You all right, Rob? Bearing up ok?' asked Harry, hugging his nephew as he rose to greet him.

'Not really, Uncle. The doctors have just left. Mum's cancer's spreading aggressively, they're just trying to make her comfortable now. She's only a week or two left at most,' said Rob, his eyes watering and his lip trembling slightly as he fought against the tears.

'It's all right, son, I know,' said Harry hugging him again.

'Does Danny know?' asked Harry.

'I've left word at Hereford. They're trying to get hold of his unit, wherever they are.'

'Ok, remember, any problem call me. The hospital bill is taken care of, right, but if you need money for the house or anything, you just ask, ok?' said Harry, his voice stirring Maureen from her sleep.

'Harry,' she said weakly.

'All right, Sis, how you doing?' he asked, taking her frail hand as Rob turned away so his mother couldn't see the tears in his eyes.

'I'm just gonna get a drink. Do you want one, Harry?' he asked.

'I'm ok, Rob, I can't stay long,' Harry replied. Rob nodded and disappeared down the corridor.

'Good kid, that. He's a credit to you, Sis.'

'I'm proud of both of them,' she said, squeezing his hand. Her face turned serious.

'Promise me you'll look out for them when I'm gone,' she said holding his gaze, her eyes searching for the confirmation she suddenly needed to hear.

'Course I will, Sis, you don't need to ask,' replied Harry, putting his other hand on top of hers to comfort her. She smiled and sank back into the puffed-up pillows, her body seeming to almost disappear.

'I'm sorry, I've gotta get going now. I'll try to get in tomorrow, Sis,' he said as Maureen nodded. Her eyes were already closing as she nodded back to a medicated sleep.

FIVE

Tired and hungry after a long flight, Danny Pearson strolled out of passport control into the arrivals hall at London Heathrow's Terminal 5. He squinted at the low summer sun as it threw its blinding orange rays through the windows of the terminal building. Carrying nothing but his frayed old army backpack, he crossed the shiny polished floor and exited into warm evening air.

Home sweet home.

Dressed in jeans and a light canvas jacket that hid a shrunken-in-the-wash t-shirt straining over his muscular build, he felt in his pocket for his vibrating phone and smiled as he answered.

'Scotty, where are you mate?' he said peering up the approach road.

'Just coming, old chap. Some jobsworth policeman read me the riot act about the no waiting zone. I've had to go around the block. Now coming,' said Danny's best friend, Scott Miller.

As soon as he was off the phone the throaty gurgle of a sports car echoed along the approach road. A red Porsche came into view pulling up beside him. His friend's grinning face and floppy, sandy-coloured hair made him smile as he opened the door and climbed in.

'Good to see you, Scotty boy, thanks for this,' he said, barely closing the door before Scott pulled away hard onto the exit road.

'Really not a problem, old boy. Emma's at her sister's for the foreseeable, I'm afraid, so you can stay as long as you want,' replied Scott, a little melancholy.

'Oh really? Sorry, Scott. I didn't know you two were having problems.'

'If I'm honest, I don't think it was ever destined to work. We've been arguing a lot lately. I took on a young Japanese student with some intern work to help towards her university degree. Unfortunately, Emma came home and caught me and the intern helping each other out in the bedroom,' said Scott, raising a cheeky smile.

'Jesus, you never could keep it in your pants.'

'Yes, well, anyway. Getting back to you, old man, how long are you back for?'

'I'm out, mate. Finished. My heart isn't in it anymore,' said Danny, his face suddenly hardening and his eyes far away.

'Does Rob know?' asked Scott, trying to keep the conversation moving.

'Eh, no. I'll go and see Mum tomorrow and catch up with Rob afterwards.'

'Your mum will be pleased to see you. She's got a lot worse over the last couple of weeks,' said Scott, his eyes tearing up a little. He'd known Maureen since he, Danny and Rob had been at primary school. He'd spent more time at their house than his own.

'Yeah, I know,' said Danny as the car went into an awkward silence. Shaking himself out of self-pity Danny grinned and lightened the mood.

'Ok, what we having then, Scotty boy? Chinese, Indian, fish and chips? Your choice, mate, I'm paying.'

'You getting your wallet out? Now that's an offer I can't refuse. I'll go for Chinese then,' said Scott grinning. He dropped down a gear and hit the gas, pushing them back in their seats as he powered down the M4 towards central London and his home in Kingston upon Thames. Forty minutes later Danny was clearing old pizza boxes off Scott's table, while Scott found the last two clean plates in the cupboard for the takeout.

'Bloody hell, Scott, how long ago did Emma move out?'

'Last week, old man, why?' asked Scott, puzzled.

Danny looked up from shovelling more cans and wrappers into a bin bag.

'Really!' he said, shaking his head with a grin.

The childhood friends ate and drank until jet lag and beer got the better of Danny. Yawning, he retired to Scott's spare room. As his head hit the pillow he realised it was the first time in ages that he'd not thought about his wife and child, the accident that killed them or his terminally ill mother. It was a welcome respite, if only short-lived.

SIX

A few hundred metres back from London Bridge on the
busy A3 sat Silk & Lace gentleman's club. Its front was
adorned with shiny blacked-out windows and black
painted brickwork. The shadow of London's prominent
skyscraper, The Shard, reached the pavement outside, its
point showing the way in. The Silk & Lace signage hung
garishly over the entrance, its large illuminated silver
letters giving the impression of legitimacy. In reality it
masked a multitude of illegal activities hidden behind its
dark façade. Viktor Volkov sat in his office on the third
floor. He spun his vodka around the ice in his glass
before downing it in one. A knock at the office door
caused his brooding eyes to flick up.

'Come!' he shouted, thumping his empty glass down
on the desk. He'd been in a foul mood since his brother's

call, and his head was banging after a cocaine-filled afternoon.

Dimitri entered, pushing two of their drug runners ahead of him. The two could barely stand. Their clothes were torn and covered with pavement dirt, white stripes of cocaine, and dried blood from their swollen, cut and bruised faces.

'What the fuck is this?' shouted Viktor sitting forward, his eyes blazing.

'Sorry, Mr Volkov. Five of Harry Knight's boys jumped us. They gave us a beating and took our money. One of them ripped the bags open and poured all the gear over us. They told us to fuck off over our side of the river and never try coming back,' said the larger of the two men sheepishly, trying to avoid eye contact with Viktor.

'What? Motherfucker!' shouted Viktor, standing and launching his empty glass at the wall behind them. As the shards dropped to the ground he exploded into a rant of Russian obscenities. When he'd finished he returned to his chair and sat. His cold blue eyes stared murderously at the two nervous men.

'Where did this happen?'

'Just down from Soho Square, Mr Volkov,' the smaller man said through split swollen lips.

The tension was insufferable. Viktor had a reputation for unpredictability and the two men knew it. It was rumoured he had a gun in his desk and had killed people just for looking at him funny.

'Ok, fuck off and clean yourselves up,' he finally said.

The two men sighed with relief and turned to leave. Halfway through the office door, they froze in terror as Viktor spoke again.

'Hey, you two fuckups, you talk about this to no one, da? No one. You understand?'

His voice had returned to its usual menacing, cold, calm self. They turned to acknowledge Viktor with a nod, quickly spotting the arrival of a gun sitting on his desk in front of him.

'No, Dimitri, you stay,' he said as the two men limped out, shutting the door behind them.

'We will take care of this, Dimitri. I do not want this getting back to my brother, am I clear?' said Viktor sliding the gun back into the draw slowly, without taking his eyes off Dimitri as he did so.

'Of course, Viktor, what did you have in mind?' asked Dimitri, trying to sound as calm as possible. He kept his relief in check as Viktor reached back into the drawer and brought a bottle of vodka out, slamming it on the desk between them. Viktor picked up the phone and called down to the bar.

'Bring me some ice and two glasses,' he barked.

'Sit, Dimitri, sit. I have an idea.'

A knock at the door caused him to shout once more. 'Come!'

A pretty but nervous young blond girl entered with a small bucket of ice and two tumblers on a tray.

'I have your ice and glasses, Mr Volkov,' she said timidly, the tray shaking slightly in her hands.

Viktor's eyes softened and his sky-blue irises sparkled as she put the tray on the desk.

'Is no need to be nervous, my dear. You're new here. What's your name?' he asked, emphasising his thick Russian accent for effect as he flashed her a wide smile of perfect white teeth.

'Tanya, sir. I started this week on the bar.'

'Mm, Tanya, thank you. That will be all for now,' he said, his eyes never leaving her trim figure as she left.

The second she was gone his face hardened and his eyes narrowed, darting their focus back to Dimitri.

'When is Knight's bare knuckle fight on?'

'It's on this Friday night,' said Dimitri sitting back in the chair, trying to relax. As cousins, he and Viktor were similar in appearance, both strong and fit, with classic Russian looks.

'Friday, good. When they are all at the fight, we make a visit to his beloved pub, eh? Send him a message of our own,' said Viktor, pouring large measures of vodka into the tumblers. He shovelled his fist into the ice bucket and threw some into each glass before passing Dimitri a tumbler.

'I like it, Cousin, we will show Harry-fucking-Knight they can not push us around,' said Dimitri raising his glass.

'Nostrovia.'

'Nostrovia,' replied Viktor, returning the gesture.

They both threw their heads back, downing the drinks in one before banging them back on the table. Relaxing, the two men grinned at each other. Viktor picked up the bottle and filled the glasses again.

SEVEN

Rolling over in the semi-light of early morning, Danny stared waiting for his eyes to adjust to the gloom. It was only half five, but his head was in some other time zone. He was wide awake and already deciding to blow away the cobwebs and go for a run. Running had always helped him clear his head, and right now he needed to push his swirling montage of thoughts back behind the floodgates. Images of his terminally ill mum floated around ones of twisted metal and his departed wife and son. With the gates opened, the horrors of combat missions seeped into the mix.

I need to move, to push myself. To bury them deep down.

Pulling shorts and a t-shirt out of his rucksack, he dressed and left Scott's into the cool morning air. He ran steadily into the centre of Kingston to warm up before opening up, faster and faster, pushing the machine to the max. He crossed over the river by Hampton Court Road, stopping at the far end of the bridge with his lungs fit to burst. He paced up and down sucking the air in with large gulps. He placed his hands on the railings and looked down at the Barge Walk. It followed the riverbank, disappearing out of sight as the river meandered around a bend. With his heart rate returning to normal he took in the picturesque house boats moored up on the bank, and the tall hedges lining the other side of the path. Beyond the hedges lay the large expanse of fields and parkland belonging to Hampton Court gardens. The palace was a mile or so away, at the end of a long tree-lined approach.

He was just about to leave when four youths on the canal path caught his eye. They'd been sitting on the backrest of a bench with their feet on the seat. Only now two of them were up, with their backs to him. They were looking at something out of his line of sight, somewhere around a bend in the path.

The hairs on the back of his neck stood up, his instinct for trouble tingling inside him. Something in their manner, tiny movements in their body language were alarming him. He couldn't see their faces past the baseball caps and hoodies, but he knew it wasn't friendly. A young woman came into view, halting as two youths gestured aggressively towards her.

Danny began to move.

'Yo, bitch, where do you think you is going, eh?' said a tall pasty youth. His wiry ginger beard and yellow teeth snarled as he talked, and his bloodshot eyes were full of menace.

'Please, let me pass,' she said, trying, but not succeeding, to sound strong and confident.

'This is our path, girl, you gotta pay to use it,' said a shorter Caribbean youth, his dreadlocks sticking out from his cap and hoodie. The other two members of the gang were still sitting on the bench, chuckling.

The woman started backing up the path away from them.

'Where are you going, bitch? I say when you leave,' said the wiry ginger haired one, as he pulled a flick knife out, pointing it at her like a finger.

The two on the bench got up, closing in on her with the others like pack animals. She froze, terrified, tears welling up as she shook her head.

'The lady will go wherever she wants to go.'

The voice from behind them made them jump and turn all at once. Seeing Danny standing there on his own brought out more pack animal bravado. Ginger Beard took point jiggling the flick knife in his hand.

'You wanna mind your own, old man. Go on, jog on, this ain't none of your biz,' he said, puffing his chest up and tilting his chin up.

'I don't think so, sonny. How about you put your little toy knife away before you hurt yourself, and let the lady pass,' said Danny smiling, his eyes focused and alert as he played out various scenarios in his head.

'Toy knife? He is dissin' you, blood. Don't be takin' that shit off him,' said the spotty, greasy-looking teen as he pulled a bigger hunting knife out of his jacket.

Danny kept walking steadily towards them, noting the fleeting confusion in their faces as he kept coming.

'Fuck off, man, or I'll cut you,' said Ginger Beard, raising his knife.

The move was short-lived. Danny grabbed Ginger's forearm with one hand and the back of his wrist with the other. Pulling the forearm out and pushing the wrist in hard, there was a loud click and Ginger let go of the knife in agony as he stared at his limp wrist in shock. Danny had already moved onto Dreadlocks before the knife hit the floor. He unleashed a lightning combination of punches to the temple and nose putting Dreadlocks out cold. As Ginger howled on the floor beside him, the other two stared in disbelief. Danny stood calmly and winked at them with a smile.

'Who's next?'

The two backed away before turning and running off up the path past the shaking woman.

'It's ok,' said Danny with a soft smile as he gestured for her to pass.

She walked between Dreadlocks and Ginger, who was cradling his wrist, whimpering; she passed him, still shaking, before stopping. A determined look came across her face as she turned and kicked Ginger's wrist as hard as she could, causing him to howl even louder.

'Thank you,' she said as she hurried past.

Danny noticed some little bags had fallen out of Dreadlocks' pocket. Bending down he picked one up. A dubious white powder was packed inside. The bag itself had a little red sticker on it with a yellow star over a yellow *V*. It was like an old Russian flag, with the *V* where the hammer and sickle would have been. He searched Dreadlocks' pockets, pulling out more bags, this time with pills in. Looking further he found a fat roll of money with an elastic band around it.

'You fucking leave that alone, you fuck,' said Ginger Beard grunting through the pain.

Danny tucked the roll of notes in his shorts pocket before scooping up the bags and dropping them in the river.

'No, no, no! Fuck! You're a dead man. Wait until the Russian hears about this. He'll find you and—,'

Danny grabbed him by the throat, shutting him up in mid-sentence.

'If I were you, I'd change my line of work. Smarten yourself up, make something of yourself,' said Danny gripping tighter until Ginger Beard's eyes rolled back in his head and he passed out. He picked the flick knife off the floor and threw it in the river after the drugs. After checking Ginger's pockets, he found more drug bags, money, and a mobile. He tossed the gear on the floor and dialled 999 on Ginger's phone.

'Hello, which service do you require?'

'Police, please come quick, I'm on Barge Walk, Kingston. There are two men selling drugs and threatening people.'

Danny dropped the phone without hanging up, and without further thought, turned and continued his run. The incident was instantly forgotten—he didn't consider it serious enough to dwell on.

EIGHT

After sliding silently into Scott's, Danny showered and dressed. With his unruly dark hair still dripping onto his shoulders, he followed the smell of bacon and descended the stairs. He chuckled at the sound of Scott singing badly in the kitchen.

'Morning Scotty.'

'Morning, old boy. Bacon butty?'

'Top man, I'll make a brew,' Danny replied, clicking on the kettle.

'How was the run this morning? Good to be back?'

'Yeah, it was good, mate. Even met some of the locals,' said Danny with a little smile to himself.

With breakfast finished, he caught a lift part-way with Scott on his way to work. Scott dropped Danny near The Shard, a short walk from London Bridge Tube station. The capital was buzzing with the morning rush.

Cars crawled bumper-to-bumper, the occasional horn beeping as drivers released some of their frustration. Crowds of the capital's workers merged with crowds of tourists and day-trippers as they fought for pavement space. Danny loved the hustle and energy of London with its historic, picturesque buildings side-by-side with the new steel and glass skyscrapers. He turned towards the Tube station and glanced at some graffiti in a doorway that caught his eye.

A red square with a yellow star, above a yellow V just like the drug packages.

He took a mental picture before entering the Tube station. He rode the Underground as it shook and screeched through a couple of changes to his destination. After a short walk from the station Danny eased the door of the hospital room open. His mum was sitting up in bed, pillows supporting her shrinking frame. Harry sat holding her hand as he talked to her. She turned towards the door taking a second to register Danny's arrival. Her face lit up with the light of her former self.

'Daniel,' she said reaching out for him.

'Hello, Mum.'

He walked over and kissed her on the cheek.

'Harry,' said Danny with a nod.

'Hiya, kid, nice to see you back. I'll go get myself some air, let you catch up with your mother,' said Harry, patting Danny on the shoulder as he left.

'How you doing, Mum?'

'All the better for seeing you. Does Robert know you're back?' said Maureen, placing a hand on Danny's cheek.

'No, I got back last night and stayed at Scott's. I'm going to see Rob when I leave here.'

'Good, your brother's going to need you when I'm gone,' said Maureen, looking straight into his eyes.

He wanted to tell her not to be stupid, that everything would be all right, but he knew it wasn't, and acknowledged it with a simple nod.

They talked for a while before Harry returned, closely followed by a nurse.

'Sorry, everybody, Maureen needs some rest now.'

'Ok, I'll be back tomorrow, Mum,' said Danny, kissing her goodbye.

'I'll come and see you as soon as I get a minute, Sis,' said Harry, leaving with Danny.

'I'll give you a lift home, son,' he said in the corridor.

As they walked out of the hospital Harry's Bentley drew silently up beside them. Tom hopped out of the driver's seat and scooted round to open the door for Harry.

'Thanks, Tom,' he said, sliding across to let Danny in.

As Danny went to get in the car he noticed two youths on a moped as they bumped up on the pavement around a hundred metres away. He couldn't see their faces through the mirrored visors on their bright zigzag-patterned crash helmets. The hairs on the back of his neck stood on end. By their build and clothes they were late teens or wiry early twenties. Danny's focus in their direction caused them to move off. He hadn't paused long and got in the car without alerting the others. Danny was in no doubt they'd been watching Harry's car.

'Can you take me to Maureen's house please, Tom?' said Harry, settling back in the seat.

'Ok, Boss.'

'So how long you back for, son?' said Harry turning to Danny.

'I'm out, Harry. I quit the regiment.'

'Christ, really? You got any plans now you're back?'

'Not really. An old friend of mine left a few years back and set up a security company in the city. He always said if I need a job to look him up,' said Danny, his eyes scanning for the moped as they talked. There was no sign of it.

'Look, I've got an event tomorrow night. Why don't you come and work the door for me? Earn a bit of cash and help me out.'

Harry didn't really need Danny, but family was family and you looked after your own.

'Thanks, Harry, yeah that'd be good,' Danny replied, happy to take the work to keep his mind off things.

Turning onto Walthamstow High Street, Harry told Tom to pull over by a parade of shops.

'Just got to get your Auntie Lou some flowers,' he said, winking to Danny.

'You the army boy, then?' said Tom, his narrow staring eyes and broken nose visible in the rear-view mirror.

Hello, someone wants a pissing contest.

'Not anymore. You the driver boy, then?' said Danny smiling back to the eyes in the mirror.

'I do many things for Mr Knight, mate, so watch your lip.'

'Oh, I'm sorry. You clean the car and fill it up as well,' said Danny smiling outwardly, while inside his anger and frustration from the past and his mum's future was growing beyond containment.

'You piss-taking little shit. You wanna step out of the motor, and I'll show you what else I do,' said Tom, flushed and glaring at him.

'Why the hell not?' said Danny, fired up and ready to blow.

They both got out. Tom stormed round the car fronting up to Danny. The two of them were just about to go at it when Harry's voice boomed over them.

'Oi! Fucking pack it in, you two. I leave you alone for two minutes and you start acting like a right couple of pricks.'

Tom moved back to the driver's side, still fuming as he clenched and unclenched his fists. Danny, while looking outwardly calm, moved to get back into the car. He spotted the moped again over Harry's shoulder, tucked in a side street, the riders peeping around a hedge in his direction.

'What the fuck was that all about?' asked Harry.

'Sorry, Boss,' said Tom sheepishly.

'Danny?' he asked, looking across at him.

'Err, what? Oh, Harry, is there any reason why anyone would be following you?' he said, his face rigid, eyes locked firmly forward through the front windscreen.

'Who? Where? What did they look like?' asked Harry, looking aimlessly around.

'Two lads on a moped, scruffy sports clothing, crash helmets with mirrored visors. They were at the hospital and then up the road looking around a hedge. They're gone now.'

Harry stared intensely forward to where Danny said they had been. After a long minute, he shared a knowing look with Tom. It was short but Danny caught it.

'Nothing to worry about, son, probably just kids eyeing up the motor. Drive on, Tom, let's get going,' said Harry unconvincingly.

Danny let it go and sat back for the rest of the journey, trying to get a grip on his inner turmoil. They pulled up outside the house he grew up in. He thanked Harry and ignored the sneer from Tom. As they drove off he knocked at the door of the old four-bedroom Georgian house.

NINE

Danny smiled as a skinny silhouette appeared from the other end of the hall. The outline grew larger until it filled the multi-coloured stained glass in the old front door. It opened a crack and Rob's questioning face peeped around its edge, a grin spread across it as the penny dropped a second later.

'About bloody time you turned up,' he said, throwing the door open and giving his brother a hug.

'All right, squirt, keep your hair on,' Danny chuckled as the two of them went inside.

The look and smell of the hall with the creaking of the floorboards transported him back through the years to his childhood. Happy memories of Scott, Rob and him playing as kids. They went through to the kitchen. Danny went to sit at the table as Rob clicked on the kettle.

'I wouldn't sit in that one, the leg's loose. One good lean and you'll be on the floor in pieces.'

Danny moved seats and the two of them fell into an awkward silence, neither of them wanting to start the conversation about their mum.

'How you bearing up, Rob? You all right?' Danny finally said.

His brother finished making the drinks and sat at the table. He looked tired as he spoke.

'I can't lie. It's been tough. She'll be made up to see you. When did you get back?'

'Last night. Scott picked me up. I went to see Mum this afternoon and met Uncle Harry there. He gave me a lift.'

'Harry's been there most days. He's been great—I don't know what I would have done without him,' said Rob getting up at the sound of the doorbell.

When Rob answered, Danny could hear a woman's voice and was glad to see Rob return with his girlfriend, Tina.

'Danny! Lovely to see you back,' she said, moving round the table to give him a big hug and a kiss on the cheek.

Danny liked Tina—she was always upbeat and the two of them were good together.

'All right, love, good to see you too,' said Danny, happy to side-step conversation about his mum's cancer.

He watched with a big grin as Tina cupped Rob's face, giving him a big kiss and causing him to blush.

'How much leave have you got, Danny?'

'I'm not going back, Rob. I'm out, bro.'

'Out? What, you quit?' said Rob, shocked.

'Yep,' said Danny bluntly. The look on his face told them he didn't want to talk about it.

'Why don't I give Scott a ring, get him to bring takeout and beers? We can all have a catch up,' Danny finally said, changing the subject.

'That'd be great. I haven't seen Scott much since his wife left him.'

Danny laughed out loud.

'Great bunch we are. All we need now is a psychiatrist and a bottle of anti-depressants and we can start the party.'

TEN

DCI Nichola Swan pulled her Mini into the yard at Kingston police station. The brakes squeaked as she stopped, temporarily drowning out the noise of the rattly engine. She grabbed a file from between the empty coffee cups and McDonald's wrappers and got out. In contrast to the inside of her car, Swan's appearance was immaculate. She wore a crisp white blouse under a navy blue trouser suit and flat, shiny black shoes. She was slim and had inherited her mother's Moroccan features— large brown eyes and long shiny black hair, tied neatly back in a ponytail. She entered the station and approached the desk sergeant.

'Hi, Nick. I believe you've got a Trevor Bailey in, escorted back from the hospital?'

'Yes, Ma'am, and he's been complaining ever since he arrived,' said Nick dryly.

'Could I have him brought up to an interview room, please? I'll be upstairs if you can call us when he's ready.'

Swan smiled as Nick buzzed her through from reception into the station.

'Yes, Ma'am, I'll get him brought up.'

The upstairs operations room was almost empty. Unless there was a major incident only a skeleton crew worked the evening shift. She spotted DCI Jonathan Cripp hunched over his PC terminal and made her way over.

'Evening, Jon. Found anything new?' she said, peering over his shoulder at some CCTV footage. 'Is that him?' she added.

'Yep, that's him, Mrs Temple's knight in shining armour,' said Cripp flicking the footage back and forward.

'Or a manic attacker according to Mr Bailey. Any idea who he is?' said Swan, squinting at a blurry blown up image.

'Nah, maybe he's a martial arts nut or amateur boxer. We could try the local gyms or clubs.' Cripp shrugged. It wasn't exactly high on the priority list. The powers-that-be wouldn't sanction valuable man hours to investigate an assault on two known dealers under dubious circumstances.

The phone rang on the office internal line.

'Thank you,' said Cripp, putting it back down.

'Our upstanding citizen, Mr Bailey, is in interview room one. Shall we?'

'Yep, let's get this over with,' said Swan sighing and making for the stairs.

Trevor Bailey sat slouched, legs apart in his scruffy skinny jeans. His head was down with his eyes obstructed by a baseball cap and hoodie. He cradled his freshly bandaged wrist as he painfully flexed his swollen blackish-blue fingers. His eyes moved up from under his cap at the sound of the door opening.

'Bout fucking time. Why'd you bring me back here? I ain't done nuttin,' he said angrily through his ratty ginger beard, his bloodshot eyes burning defiantly.

'Calm down, Mr Bailey. We just want to ask you a few questions.'

Swan and Cripp took a seat opposite and pressed the record button on the interview recorder.

'Interview of Trevor Bailey commencing at 19:25. Present are DCI Nichola Swan and DC Jonathan Cripp,' said Swan, opening the folder.

'Right, Mr Bailey. Now your wrist has been attended to, can you run us through the alleged assault on yourself and Lenard Timms,' said Cripp sitting back, his arms crossed and face expressionless.

'Yeah, well, this geezer comes along the path by the river and stops me and Lenny. He pulls a knife and tells us to give him all our money and phones. Lenny tells him to fuck off, and he goes ballistic. He knocks Lenny clean out. I wrestled the knife off him but done me wrist in fighting him off. I ripped his pocket in the scuffle and that's when all the drugs fell out. He ran off scared and then you lot turned up,' said Trevor, his face twitching as he avoided direct eye contact.

'Well done. Quite the proverbial hero aren't we, Mr Bailey,' said Swan, pausing after she spoke to let the tension in the room grow.

'Eh, yeah. I was just doin' my bit, you know,' he said with a slouched shrug.

'Hmm, that's odd because I've got a statement from Mrs Temple. She says you and three of your mates stopped her passing and threatened her. She also says your attacker asked you to let her pass, and you and your gang threatened him with knives. He knocked Lenard out and disarmed you while your two mates ran off. When he'd finished with you two, he let her through and on her way. It doesn't sound much like a mugging, does it, Mr Bailey?'

Swan finished talking and sat motionless. They could almost feel Trevor's discomfort as he fidgeted in the chair.

'Nah, nah, that's bollocks, man, she's off her nut. You ain't got no proof.'

The interview door opening interrupted Trevor's rant. A man in a cheap creased suit entered. His shirt buttons strained against his podgy midriff, as he smoothed his greasy hair back, trying to catch his breath.

'David Wilkins. I'm Mr Bailey's solicitor,' he said, sitting next to Trevor. 'Look, I've been fully briefed. After suffering a brutal attack, my client has provided you with a full statement. Unless you are going to charge him, I suggest you release him immediately,' said Wilkins, gesturing for Trevor to get up.

Swan and Cripp looked at each other before standing up.

'Interview terminated at 19:45. Mr Bailey you are free to go. For now.'

She closed her folder and walked out past Trevor as he smirked triumphantly. Back upstairs Swan threw her hands up in frustration.

'Agh, that little shit. I'd like to know who paid that sleazy solicitor to turn up this time of night.'

'Ah, Mr Wilkins, he's been here rather a lot lately, representing various questionable characters over extortion, prostitution and drug possession. The rumour mills have it that Mr Wilkins and his clients are on the payroll of Viktor Volkov,' said Cripp, picking his coat off the back of the chair.

'Viktor Volkov, the Russian with the lap dancing club?' she said following him down the stairs.

'That's him.'

'Hmm. I'd really like to find our mysterious jogger,' she said as they exited into the car park.

'I'll put the word about. No point talking to the super. He won't sanction any man hours for it,' he said shrugging.

'Thanks, Jon, I know. You have a good night, I'll see you tomorrow,' she said, opening the creaky door of her scruffy Mini.

ELEVEN

The next morning all three of them sat at the kitchen table hugging hot coffee, with thick heads and subdued conversation. The night had been just like old times. Danny and Scott would leave the wives at home, pick up Rob and hit the pubs. Since Danny lost his family, nights of laughter and banter along with a heavy consumption of beer had been few and far between. Tina had enjoyed seeing the tension lift from Rob's face, if only for a while. She'd retired early, leaving them to it and left for work before the boys got up. Taking the initiative, Rob prepared a standard British hangover cure of a fried breakfast. Sobered up and full up, Scott gave them a lift to the hospital. He parked in the drop off bay and descended into fits of laughter as Danny tried to get his sizeable frame out of the Porsche's tiny rear seats. Rob pulled his arm and Scott pushed him from inside.

'Jesus, how much did you pay for that bloody thing?'

'If you weren't such a fat bastard, you'd have got out easily,' replied Scott grinning.

'Yeah, you have put a few pounds on, bruv,' said Rob chipping in.

'You know I could kill you both without breaking a sweat,' said Danny with a mock karate chop.

'Nah, you'd need us to tie your shoelaces first. See you later, caveman,' said Scott, gunning the Porsche out of the car park.

'He's such an arsehole. Come on, let's go see Mum,' he said, patting Rob on the back.

They found her awake, propped up on pillows, watching daytime TV. Her face lit up when she saw them.

'My boys! I'm so happy to see you together.'

Overcome with emotion at seeing both of them she broke down in tears.

'Hi, Mum,' said Danny, wiping her tears away and kissing her on the cheek.

'Don't upset yourself, Mum,' said Rob.

'It's ok, I'm just happy, Rob,' she said touching his face.

They talked as the afternoon rolled in. Before long Danny had to leave to go to Harry's for the evening's work. Riding the Underground once more, Danny walked through the affluent St John's Wood area of London which was home to celebrities and the city's money men, and the odd gangster. When he reached a high rendered wall and large oak gates, he pressed the intercom on the wall.

'Yes,' came a gruff metallic voice.

'I'm here to see Harry.'

'And who are you?'

'Danny Pearson.'

The intercom clicked off and the gates smoothly opened to reveal the largest house on the street. There was a lot of activity at the house. The drive was full of Range Rovers and Mercedes and Harry's Bentley. Several black-suited men milled around outside, some older, some early twenties. Tough school of hard knocks kind of guys, they eyed him with suspicion, like they did anyone outside their circle. Danny had already clocked the older ones' jackets, the left arms hanging a fraction further out than the right, the slightest of bulge of the cloth over a concealed gun. He wasn't completely surprised. He'd grown up with the stories of Harry Knight's rise from the poor streets of Stratford. One of his men indicated for Danny to put his arms out and patted him down for weapons. His hands were massive with fingers like sausages.

'Leave it out, Ron, that's my nephew,' came Louise's voice shouting from the front door.

Danny grinned, walking past Ron. Louise threw her arms around him, giving him a big kiss on the cheek.

'Let me look at you. You look more like your father every time I see you. Come in. May's here; she'd love to see you,' she said, dragging him by the hand.

'Ok, Lou, but I'm supposed to be doing a job for Harry.'

'Never mind about him. He's busy on the phone checking the bookies' takings. He'll be at least half an hour.'

'Danny! Dad said you were back,' said May, running across the kitchen to throw her arms around him.

'Whatcha, Titch. How are you?'

May was the same age as Danny. He'd been more like a big brother growing up. He'd looked after her through school and through their teens until he joined the army at eighteen.

'I'm good, thanks. I've gone back to college to do my art degree,' she said as bubbly and happy as he last remembered her.

'I'm glad to see you're doing something deep and meaningful with your life,' said Danny chuckling.

'Shut up, you big idiot.'

They talked for a while until Harry came searching out the chatter.

'Ah, good, you're here. Ready to go, son?' said Harry, giving Louise a kiss on his way past.

'Yeah, but I haven't got a suit or uniform,' said Danny, pointing to his dark jeans and white shirt. It was the closest thing he could find to formal wear.

'That's ok, son. I just want you to walk around the crowd. Just keep it low key and keep your eyes open for anyone stepping out of line.'

Harry waited by the door as Danny tried to get away from his aunt and cousin.

'God's sake, Lou, leave the boy alone, we've gotta go,' said Harry, his patience eventually wearing thin.

Riding in the back of the Bentley with Harry, they were tucked behind a Range Rover with two cars following them, full of Harry's men.

'Is everything ok, Harry, no business problems?'

Danny looked Harry straight in the eye, with a *don't bullshit me* look on his face.

'It's nothing to worry about. We've been having a little bother with some dickhead south of the river,' said Harry, dismissing it casually.

'Right. It's a big night and I don't want any little toerag spoiling it,' he said, changing the subject, as the fight venue came into view.

TWELVE

They parked the cars in the yard around the back of the closed down Plumb City warehouse. It was plain on the outside: grey breeze block walls, topped with a large, blue, corrugated metal structure. Moving round to the entrance doors, Danny was impressed at the transformation. Drapes hung either side of the doors, and they rolled a red carpet out under posts and ropes to guide the expectant guests in. A large printed canvas hung over the old faded Plumb City sign above the entrance, boldly advertising the charity event with a list of sponsors. Tom had taken his place by the door next to another of Harry's guys. They straightened up and puffed out their chests as Bob came out of the venue. He inspected them with a frown before giving them a nod of approval. He turned to face Danny, giving him a wink when he had his back to Tom.

'Everything set, Bob?' asked Harry.

'All set, Boss. Nice to see you back, son,' said Bob to Danny.

'Tom, get Danny a headset and radio, he'll be working the room in case anyone steps out of line,' he said over his shoulder, causing Tom to scowl at Danny. They held each other's gaze for a few seconds longer, until Tom eventually broke off and disappeared inside.

'What time does it all kick off, Bob?' said Danny casually.

Bob had worked for Harry for as long as Danny could remember. He used to take them to school and buy them sweets when they were kids.

'They'll start arriving in about half an hour, with the first fights starting at eight.'

Moving inside the warehouse, the interior was far more impressive than Danny expected. In the centre stood the boxing ring with a full lighting rig above it. Surrounding the ring were three rows of VIP tables. Seating twelve around their large black table-clothed tops, they sat on newly laid black carpet. Set up behind a barrier beyond the tables, lay the general viewing area complete with bar and food-serving area.

'Hell of a setup for a charity night, Harry,' said Danny, taking it all in.

'Er, yeah, about that. At the end of the night there's a rather special fight,' said Harry, fixing Danny with a curious look.

'Special, as in…?'

'Bare knuckle, no rules. Is that a problem?'

'Not unless you're asking me to fight,' said Danny with a grin.

'Good lad. Look, just mooch around. See any piss heads getting out of order, use the radio and we'll escort them out, ok?' said Harry, patting Danny on the shoulder before wandering off to check on things.

The evening started well as guests slowly filled the place. Gold ticketed local businessmen and their wives filled the VIP tables. Family and friends of the amateur fighters filled the general area along with the public. After a good oiling of drinks, the expectant crowd erupted with cheers as the boxing bouts started. The local clubs shouted for their own young hopefuls as they boxed rival clubs. Danny enjoyed the matches as he moved around the crowd. He'd been an amateur boxing champion in his teens and remained unbeaten in the army. The crowd was noisy and drunk, but the atmosphere was good and everyone was in good humour.

At ten thirty the advertised headline bout came on, and after three hard-hitting rounds, ended the night. Hands were shaken as Harry thanked the clubs for coming before they made their way out with most of the public. Amongst the hundred or so select guests that remained, the atmosphere started to change as money moved around. Men with notebooks weaved through the crowd, shouting odds and taking bets. Hand signals flew this way and that as bets were verbally agreed and markers were taken.

'Ladies and gentlemen, now for the main event. In the red corner, please welcome the Essex Destroyer, Mark Benton,' said the compere as a heavy rock song blared.

A fighter strutted towards the ring, taped up knuckles held high in the air. He was short and stocky, and his pale skin glared as the bright spotlight followed him. He jumped up and stepped into the ring.

'Ladies and gentlemen, please show a massive welcome. In the blue corner, the Brixton Bruiser, Dwain Jones,' he said to another loud track as a tall black fighter strutted towards the ring, his long dreadlocks tied up behind his head. Watching by the barrier Danny felt the hairs go up on the back of his neck; he could feel someone watching him. He spun around, his eyes darting, searching through the crowd. He was about to dismiss it when he caught a fleeting glance of a face at the back of the crowd. It was just a split-second glimpse before it disappeared, and it took a few seconds to register who he'd seen.

Nicholas Snipe.

Danny moved through the crowd, working his way towards the rear. He reached the back wall, still unable to find the face from his past-—the one with the intense staring eyes and manic grin.

Several years ago, they had assigned Nicholas Snipe to Danny's SAS unit. He became more and more unstable with every mission. They eventually discharged him on psychiatric grounds, after Danny had reported him for killing an innocent villager during a mission. Danny circled the room but didn't see him again.

Maybe I imagined it. Christ, I'm seeing ghosts from the past now.

A garbled stream of communication crackled into life over his earpiece, bringing his focus back into the room. Just as he tried to hear it over the crowd, the Essex Destroyer hit the deck, KO'd. The room erupted in noise and Danny couldn't hear a thing. He jostled through the crowd and moved to the entrance to find Bob.

'They. Done Pete at t. Dog. Fuck. Russian ba—,' came a crackled message through his earpiece, not making much sense.

'What's going on, Bob?' asked Danny, reaching the door.

'Trouble. Fight's over. Let's get 'em out. We've gotta go.'

THIRTEEN

Laughing and joking as he shook hands, Harry patted the last guests on the back and urged them out the door. The second they were gone his face hardened, flushed with anger. Bob and Tom joined him as the cars pulled up out the front. Just as they were about to leave, Danny got in the Bentley.

'No, Danny, you don't need to get involved in this,' said Harry.

'I know, but I think I'll come along for the ride.'

The look on Danny's face and tone of his voice ended any objection as the cars moved off. The journey wasn't far and driving at twice the speed limit it only took them ten minutes.

The three cars braked hard at the sight of blue flashing lights surrounding the Dog-n-Duck. The second the

Bentley stopped Harry was out, marching to the pub like a bulldog after its bone.

'Sir, sir, can you wait there please? SIR!' called a policeman, hurrying from an ambulance towards Harry as he made for the pub door.

Bob, Tom, and Danny stood back at the cars with the other lads, taking in the damage.

'Fuck off, son. This is my gaff and I'm going in,' said Harry, throwing his arm out and pointing a warning to the young officer.

'Sir, this is a crime scene. I must ask you to stay behind the tape. I can't let you enter until the DCI and CSI clear the site. Two men have been seriously assaulted here.'

Harry's mood changed instantly. His anger faded, immediately replaced by concern.

'Listen, son, my name is Harry Knight. This is my pub. Tell me who's been hurt,' Harry ordered, storming past the stammering officer before he could answer.

He reached the ambulance with the officer in tow and swung the back door open, making the paramedic jump.

'Denis, you all right, son? Where's Pete?' he asked, ignoring the police officer as he tried to pull him away.

'I'll be all right, Harry. They worked Pete over good and proper,' said Denis through split, swollen lips and a swollen, half-closed eye.

'Who was it?' said Harry, shooting a look at the officer to back off.

'It was that big fucker, Ivan, with four of Volkov's guys. He said touch any of Viktor's boys again and he'll kill you.'

The paramedic eventually protested and pushed Harry back so he could close the doors and take Denis to the hospital.

'All right, all right,' said Harry, shrugging off the persistent officer and paramedic.

'Take it easy, son. I'll take care of it.'

As the ambulance drove away, Harry moved over to Danny and Bob to look at the pub. Even from the outside you could see they'd trashed it. Most of the windows were smashed. A table was half in and out of one of them. They could see what was left of the bar through the holes, its optics and pumps were all smashed up. The pub's century-old oak-top bar was splintered with slicing V-shaped grooves, where Viktor's guys had gone at it with an axe.

'Bastard. I've gotta show that fucking Russian we're not to be messed with,' said Harry to Bob, who nodded in agreement. The group of men turned to go, only to be taken by surprise by DCI Nichola Swan and DC Jonathan Cripp standing right behind them.

'Good evening. Mr Knight isn't it?' said Swan.

'Who wants to know?'

Right on cue, Swan and Cripp held up their Metropolitan Police ID badges. Harry continued looking straight at their faces, without so much as a glance at the badges.

'Nasty business, Mr Knight. Have you got any idea what happened here?'

Swan didn't really expect a flood of co-operation. Harry Knight had a large folder back at HQ, and there was no end to the stories of how he got to run most of North London.

'How the fuck should I know? I've just got here. Why don't you two stop asking me daft fucking questions and do your fucking jobs? Find the toerags that wrecked my bar. Now if you don't mind, I'm late for a business meeting.'

Harry pushed his way past towards the car, closely followed by Bob and Danny.

'Excuse me, sir, have you been running in Kingston recently?' said Swan spotting Danny.

She couldn't be certain, but his resemblance and physique were a pretty close match to the grainy CCTV footage of the runner leaving the canal incident.

'No,' said Danny bluntly as he continued walking.

'A man fitting your description helped a young woman who was being assaulted by some youths on a canal walk.'

'Good for him.'

'The CCTV footage we have looks a lot like you.'

'I guess I've got one of those faces,' said Danny, flashing her a smile.

'I guess you have, and what name would I put to one of those faces?' she said returning his smile, displaying a row of perfect white teeth and a sparkle in her eyes that Danny couldn't help but be drawn to.

'Peter Freeman,' he said without hesitation.

In the SAS, anonymity was essential for security. If your true identity got leaked it could put you and your family at risk.

'Now that wasn't so hard, was it, Mr Freeman?' she said, their eyes locking just a little too long as Danny got back in the car.

'Tom, take me to that shithole lap dancing club of Viktor's.'

FOURTEEN

It was a quiet night at Silk & Lace. A group of celebrating middle-aged businessmen laughed and leered at a young blonde as she spun around a pole in her bra and lacy knickers. A cheer went up as she landed on her feet and squatted in ridiculously high thigh length boots. She swung her arse past their podgy faces, pausing so they could tuck money in her knicker elastic. Viktor was at the bar in good spirits. Ivan was busy relaying details of how he'd wrecked Harry's pub and beaten the landlord to a pulp. Viktor laughed and slapped Ivan on the back as they downed another shot. He'd just signalled to Tanya for more drinks when his doorman flew backwards through the foyer doors. He landed in a round booth, crashing on top of the table, sending glasses flying everywhere before ending up in a heap on the floor. Bob's intimidating bulk entered behind the other doorman whose his hands were up, with Bob's gun thrust in the back of his neck. More of Harry's boys moved into the club and fanned out around the booths. As soon as they were in place, Harry walked in through the middle. He headed towards Viktor and Ivan. Danny moved in behind him, his eyes scanning, assessing, his body unnoticeably tense, ready for action.

Without warning, Ivan lunged towards Harry, the hand behind his back reappearing with a large knife. Within a split-second, Danny reacted, leaping in front of Harry to catch Ivan's wrist. He pushed the knife high and kicked him in the balls with all his might. As Ivan doubled forward in pain, Danny head-butted him hard on the bridge of his nose, shattering cartilage and sending him to the ground in a crumpled heap. The events were only just dawning on Harry's men as Danny moved onto Viktor. He'd spotted him reaching inside his jacket for a gun. Pulling it out, Viktor pointed it at Harry for the shot. Danny was ahead of him, his mind in overdrive, seeing events in slow motion. He used his weight and forward momentum to power-punch Viktor squarely in the face. The force sent Viktor flying through the bar stools. His gun clattered across the floor. Their reactions on catch-up, Harry and Bob moved forward and grabbed Viktor, thumping him down into a private booth. Danny glanced at the group of businessmen cowering in their seats.

'You lot fuck off, you didn't see anything, ok?' he said, his face as hard as granite as he fixed them with an intense stare.

With their faces as white as sheets they shuffled quickly out of the booth and hurriedly rushed out the door, avoiding eye contact from the stares of Harry's men. At the back of the room Dimitri had seen the men enter and moved himself quietly back through the swing doors into the kitchen. He crouched down, watching through the small round window in the door to the bar.

'You will fucking pay for this,' said Viktor, spitting blood at Harry through his split lip.

Harry punched him hard in the side of his head.

'Shut up and listen, you fucking Russian bastard,' he said, grabbing Viktor by his lapels.

In the background Tom shouted at the girls and bar staff to get lost. They didn't need much convincing and scooted off out of sight.

'You ever come north of the river, let alone near one of my gaffs again, they'll be dragging your body out of the Thames. You fucking understand me?' said Harry, his face inches from Viktor's.

'Fuck you,' Viktor said, his round blue eyes staring defiantly at Harry.

'Bob.'

Harry nodded towards Viktor's arm. Bob grabbed it and forced his hand flat on the table. Harry reached down and picked up Viktor's gun. Without warning, Harry placed the barrel on the back of Viktor's hand and pulled the trigger. Viktor's face froze in disbelief, the pain registering a second later as he gritted his teeth. He cradled his hand to his chest in silence, his eyes burning defiantly as he tried not to give them the satisfaction of screaming in pain.

'No more warnings,' said Harry as he pushed the hot barrel against Viktor's forehead.

The two men locked eyes. Long tense seconds passed until Viktor gave a slow half-nod. Harry backed away, leaving a red ring imprint of the barrel on Viktor's forehead. He moved to the bar and grabbed a beer towel. After rubbing his prints off the gun, he ejected the magazine and threw it with the gun over the bar. Harry gave a nod to his men before walking out. Following behind him, they retreated from the club, backing out slowly. Viktor remained seated, his eyes blazing. Ivan was holding his nose with one hand, trying to stem the flow of blood while holding his balls with the other hand.

'Aaarrrrgh. Fuck!' shouted Viktor, getting up. He held his hand tightly to stem the blood before kicking the bar stools repeatedly in a furious rant. Dimitri emerged from the kitchen and came to his side.

'You need to go to the hospital, Viktor,' he said, trying to help.

'Where the fuck have you been?'

'I was up in the office. I thought I heard a gunshot.'

'It *was* a gunshot, you fucking idiot. I can't go to the hospital, can I? Get me that fat doctor, what's his name? you know, the one that visits Suzi at the brothel. Fucking Banks get me Banks. NOW,' shouted Viktor, wrapping a towel around his bleeding hand before reaching over the bar for a bottle of vodka.

***

The Bentley drove in convoy back over Tower Bridge, heading back towards North London. Harry put his hand on Danny's shoulder as he sat in the front passenger's seat. He moved around to look back at Harry.

'Sorry, son. You shouldn't have seen that. I didn't mean to drag you into that situation.'

'Don't worry about it,' said Danny, shrugging. He'd seen and dealt with much worse.

'Ok, but don't tell your mother or Lou, they'd both kill me,' said Harry, managing a smile.

'Fucking good job you were there, son. I've never seen anybody take someone out like that,' said Bob, slapping Danny on the back.

'You and me both,' said Harry.

Danny didn't respond but noticed Tom had stopped giving him evil looks.

FIFTEEN

The next morning started uneventfully as a morning should. Danny chatted to Rob, conveniently leaving out the events that occurred after the fight. At half eight Rob left for work while Danny washed up the breakfast things before taking a taxi to the hospital. He sat with his mum for a while, but he cut the visit short as she was in a lot of pain. The doctors had to up her pain relief and as soon as it kicked in it took her into a pain-free sleep. Danny gave her a kiss on the forehead and left. He took the Tube to Angel and emerged on Islington High Street. He searched up and down for a while, eventually finding the Greenwood Security sign he was looking for. It was above a door sandwiched between a carpet shop and a Pizza Express. He entered and climbed the bare wooden staircase.

No need for a door buzzer, he thought as the steps creaked and groaned with an echoey racket. The top opened out into a small office space with a couple of desks buried under stacks of folders and file boxes. He heard some sound emanating from a door at the rear, so he weaved his way towards it.

'That's it, you've got it. Pull the big one, Trish,' came Paul Greenwood's voice.

'I am pulling. It's not coming out,' replied a woman through a strained grunt.

'Am I disturbing something? I can come back later,' said Danny with a chuckle. All he could see was the shapely rear end of a woman on her knees, sticking out from under Paul's desk.

Paul's head sprung up from the far side with a start, as Trisha jumped, banging her head on the underside of the desk.

'Shit,' she said emerging, rubbing the top of her head.

'Danny, you arse,' said Paul, grinning.

He dropped the computer leads they'd been trying to sort out and rushed over to shake Danny's hand.

'Are you all right, err...' said Danny to Trisha, barely containing his amusement as she stood upright.

'I'll live. I'm Trisha,' she said, seeing the funny side as she returned his smile.

'Danny. Pleased to meet you.'

Paul moved a box off a chair and waved him over.

'Grab a seat. As you can see, we're not quite sorted yet.'

'As long as I can find the kettle, I'll make a drink. Tea or coffee, Mr…?' said Trisha.

'Pearson.'

Paul perched on the desk corner, his face turning serious. He placed a hand on Danny's shoulder.

'How are you holding up, ok? It will take time to adjust to life after the regiment,' he said, pausing for a moment before speaking again.

'I'm sorry to hear about your mum. If there's anything I can do…'

If it had been anyone but Paul, he would have wanted to know how he knew about the regiment and his mum's illness. But he'd known Paul for years, from back when he was an intelligence officer—and an extremely well connected one at that. Whitehall, the MOD, MI6 and government officials, Paul knew them all.

'I'm not about to top myself if that's what you mean,' said Danny with as much a response as he wanted to go into.

Paul smiled. He knew Danny wasn't the opening-up type, so changed the subject.

'So, you're after some work?'

'I will be soon. I've gotta be around for mum and Rob for what little time she's got left.'

'Yes, I totally understand.'

An awkward silence fell on the room again. It was gratefully broken by Trisha returning with three odd coffee mugs.

'Thank you, Trish. Right then, on the work front, once this place is straight and you're ready I've got plenty of work—security escorts, private protection, venue security—take your pick.'

'Yeah, that'd be great, I'd really appreciate it, mate,' said Danny raising his coffee cup in a salute.

Paul explained how his client list was expanding and how he could do with Danny's expertise. Danny eventually got up to leave. When he got to the door he suddenly had a thought and turned.

'You ever heard of a guy called Viktor Volkov?'

'Viktor Volkov, he's a nasty piece of work with Russian Mafia roots. Drugs, prostitution, gambling, and it's rumoured people trafficking. Why do you ask?' said Paul, his interest piqued.

'Eh, no reason. I just heard his name mentioned.'

'Hmm ok. Keep in touch and when you're ready, come and see me about work,' said Paul, rather unconvinced at Danny's reply. They shook hands and he left.

'Bye, Trisha, nice to meet you,' he said on his way out.

'You too,' she said with a smile that didn't go unnoticed.

SIXTEEN

Deep in the heart of New Scotland Yard, Swan and
Cripp stood in the Serious Crime Squad's incident room.
Pictures of Viktor Volkov and Harry Knight had been
placed on either side of the notice boards. They drew
arrows in several directions linking the two pictures to
more photos of Viktor and Harry's known associates.
Post-it notes with ever-changing information on who was
where and what had happened were stuck under their
relevant pictures.

'I don't like this, Jon. Too much is happening to be a
coincidence,' she said, sticking a CCTV screenshot of
Bob Angel from a traffic cam near Silk & Lace. The shot
showed Bob grabbing the doormen at Viktor's club. The
next shot showed Harry and ten of his men moving
through the doors behind him. The same camera caught

Ivan limping into the club the next morning, with black eyes and a taped-up nose.

'I agree. It looks like Volkov's been making a play for North London,' said Swan standing back to take in the board.

'Yeah and Knight's having none of it.'

'I'm not sure, Jon. Is Harry Knight in Viktor's league? A dodgy property deal and a bit of illegal gambling, maybe. But he's anti-drugs and prostitution, he's just a dodgy businessman, isn't he?' said Swan shrugging.

'Maybe he is, maybe he's not. If you go back before your time the stories of his rise are legendary. Unproven murders, protection rackets and organised crime. He's cleaned up his act with a host of property, bars and clubs. But he's still a nasty bastard underneath it all.'

'Mm, if you're right this is going to escalate. We've had the tit-for-tat digs with the guys in Kingston, and my snitch says two of Volkov's runners got beaten up for dealing in Knight's pub, then last night the pub gets trashed. Later Harry takes the fight straight back to Viktor, who we haven't seen since,' she said, moving forward and tapping Danny's photo.

'I still want to know who this guy is. I ran him through the computer and got nothing on Peter Freeman.'

'Do you want me to pull him in?'

'No, what for? We've got nothing on him. We'll just have to keep digging,' said Swan, frowning at Danny's picture.

'Jon, what was it you said the other day about this guy?' she said, trying to pull the memory back.

'I don't know, erm, that he might be into martial arts or boxing.'

'Yes, that's it, but that wouldn't necessarily explain how he breezed through two thugs with knives, like it was nothing. He could be ex-military, hired muscle maybe, paid to deal with Viktor?'

'Could be, I'll get on it,' said Cripp nodding in agreement.

Swan stared at Danny's photo, thinking.

Who are you?

***

The staff and working girls at Silk & Lace had been treading on eggshells all morning. Viktor arrived an hour ago in a foul mood. His patched-up hand hurt like hell and he'd snorted a ton of coke, chased down with vodka to dull the pain. Dimitri had warned last night's staff not to talk to anyone about what happened. The consequences of what would happen if they did didn't need spelling out to them.

'What are you staring at? Get to fucking work,' Viktor yelled at the barman, who was looking at the bullet hole in the table top. The doorman from last night came out of the kitchen doors just as Viktor passed by. He looked sheepishly at the floor with his black eyes and bandaged head. Viktor stopped and glared at him.

'Have you been fucking eating again? You stupid fat prick,' shouted Victor, his blue eyes burning furiously.

'No, Viktor, I was—'

'No, Viktor, no Viktor. Shut the fuck up. What fucking good are you, anyway? Get out of my sight.'

Viktor stormed off upstairs. He ran into Ivan coming out of the toilets. Without saying anything Ivan followed Viktor, limping into the office behind him. He sat down slowly on a leather sofa. Viktor sat in his office chair behind his desk.

'You ok, Ivan? You look like shit.'

'Well, at least I've stopped pissing blood now,' said Ivan, trying to crack a smile on his painful face.

'I can't let them get away with this. If Yuri finds out about what happened, I'll never hear the end of it. I want Harry Knight dead.'

Viktor's face was deadly serious as he drained yet another vodka.

'You want me to do it?'

'No, I've a better idea. Get me the old Irish guy, O'Connell. I'll get him to do it.'

'Hmm, good idea. I'll take Karl, we'll go and find him,' said Ivan, pushing himself slowly up out of the seat. Before leaving, he fixed Viktor with a determined stare.

'The other one who did this to me. I want to kill him, that is ok. Da?'

'Knight first, then you kill him. Da. Now get me the Irishman.'

After watching Ivan leave, he instinctively picked up the phone, forgetting his injured hand. He dropped it like it was on fire, clutching his hand in intense pain. Viktor exploded in a fit of rage, hurling the empty bottle of vodka at the wall. He watched it explode into a thousand shards of glass.

Harry Knight, I will make you suffer for this.

SEVENTEEN

Several days had passed since fight night. Danny and Rob had been making their daily visits to the hospital. Maureen had been getting steadily worse each day. On their last visit, the increased medication meant she barely noticed they were there. Danny awoke at 5:32am. He had a cold chill running down his spine. A new emptiness added itself to the one occupied by his wife and child. As he got up and dressed, he heard the phone ringing downstairs, followed by Rob's hurried footsteps. He didn't hurry. There wasn't any point; he knew it was the hospital. When he came downstairs, he found Rob sitting in the kitchen looking lost.

'She's gone, Dan, Mum's dead.'

'I know, Rob,' was all Danny said as he hugged his sobbing brother.

***

DCI Nichola Swan moved through the office, throwing her coat over a chair as she looked at the situation board. Picking up a marker, she crossed out Peter Freeman and wrote Danny Pearson under Danny's CCTV picture.

'Hello, what's all this then?' said Cripp from behind her as he arrived for his shift.

'Our mystery man is Harry's nephew, Danny Pearson. You know Darren Chorley from traffic? He was up at the Elizabeth Hospital with his nan. Who should turn up? Harry Knight and Mr Mystery. Darren has a quiet word with a talkative nurse and finds out they're visiting Harry's sister, Maureen Pearson. She goes on to tell him the tall handsome young man with Harry is one of Maureen's sons, Danny Pearson. She said he turned up about a week ago.'

'Hmm, where do you think he's been hiding himself? Do you reckon he's got form? Perhaps he's fresh out of prison. I'll run him through the computer.'

'Yes, please, Jon,' said Swan, moving across to tap Viktor's picture.

'Has anyone seen Volkov since the other night?'

'Yeah, traffic clocked him tearing away from the club last night in his Ferrari, other than that he's been unusually quiet,' said Cripp, tapping away at his keyboard.

'Shame, I was hoping that low life had done us all a favour and fucked off back to Russia.'

'And there's me thinking you were a lady,' said Cripp with a smile before his face fell serious. He called Swan over.

'What is it?'

Cripp swung the monitor round for Swan to see.

'It's the report on Daniel Pearson, or rather the lack of it. He joins the army at 18, passes selection for the Commandos at 20. They award him the Victoria Cross for saving five of his unit under fire in Iraq at the age of 23. And then a big fat nothing. Top secret, Home Office classified, need-to-know shit. Until last month, where it just says, 'honourable discharge from Her Majesty's Armed Forces, no regiment, no further information.''

'Well, well, well, you are a surprise, Mr Pearson. I guess that answers the question of how he dealt with Trevor and his crew in Kingston,' said Swan as she stared at the old service photo on the computer.

'Absolutely, but it doesn't answer the question of why he's back. Is it for his dying mum or is Harry Knight recruiting enough muscle to wipe Viktor out? Either way, Mr Pearson's been involved in two altercations with Viktor's men in less than two weeks. That's a hell of a coincidence.'

'Hmm, it might be enough of a coincidence to get the super to authorise surveillance on Knight and Volkov.'

'I don't know, it's a bit of a tenuous link,' said Cripp, looking at Swan for her next move.

'Well, no time like the present,' she said, picking up the file and heading off down the corridor to the Chief Superintendent's office.

Cripp leaned back in his chair and watched Swan disappear out of sight. Picking up his mobile he made a call.

'Hi, yeah, it's me. Yes, I know who he is. No, no, I want more money, this is risky for me. Ok, I'll come to you.'

After hanging up, Cripp leaned back in his chair again to check the corridor was still clear. Satisfied no one was about, he printed out the file on Danny and slipped it into his jacket pocket.

EIGHTEEN

There was a large turnout for Maureen's funeral, despite the drizzly weather. After a short service in the small chapel at the centre of the City of London Cemetery, the family and well wishers followed the pallbearers through headstones dating back to medieval times. Her burial plot lay next to their father and her husband, Ralph. The priest said his final words and the coffin slowly lowered into the ground. Danny stood with Rob and Tina, shaking hands and thanking people as they dispersed to their cars.

Harry, Louise and May took Tina to the car, leaving the brothers to pay their final respects before moving slowly away. A scruffy blue Mini was parked over on the far side of the car park. Its window was down a few inches to stop it steaming up in the damp drizzle. No one had taken any notice. They got in their cars in a sombre mood and headed slowly out the cemetery gates. It didn't go unnoticed by Danny, nor did DCI Nichola Swan sitting in the driver's seat. By the time he and Rob had reached Harry's Bentley, Swan had started the car and driven slowly out of the cemetery. Danny turned down a lift from Rob and when he'd left with Tina, he walked across and caught Harry on his own.

'Has everything been all right since fight night, Harry?'

'Yeah, don't worry yourself about it, son, it's been dead quiet. I think that Russian wanker's finally learnt his lesson,' said Harry, forcing a smile and patting Danny on the back.

'You want a lift, son? It's pissing down.'

'No, thanks, I could do with the walk,' said Danny, oblivious to the rain.

'Ok, if you're sure. Look after yourself and don't be a stranger,' he said, climbing in the driver's seat. May waved to Danny sadly from the rear as they pulled away. He gave a single wave back and walked out the cemetery gates. Crossing the road he entered the parkland of Wanstead Flats. His body felt numb and his mind foggy. He walked and walked. He had no thoughts of where he was going—he just wanted to keep moving.

NINETEEN

On the following Friday as the day was turning into night, staff arrived and clocked into Knight's nightclub. Preparations were under way for the start of a busy weekend shift. Harry walked around checking the club as he always did.

'Suzy, love, can you give the tables in the V.I.P area another going over?' said Harry softly to one of the cleaners.

'Ok, Harry,' she said, looking up from her hoovering.

'Thanks,' he shouted behind him as he disappeared behind the bar.

He was feeling a little more positive today. It had been a few days since Maureen's funeral, and although he missed her terribly, he was glad she was no longer in pain. He'd had everyone keeping an eye out for Viktor and his men, but no one had seen any sign of them north of the river.

'Evening, Stuart. Did the drinks delivery come in ok today?' he said to his bar manager.

'Yeah, the two new lads put it all away,' said Stuart while continuing to fill up the drinks fridges.

'They getting on all right?' asked Harry. He liked to show an interest in all his staff.

'Yeah, they're good, Harry, nice couple of lads.'

Spotting Bob, Harry waved him over towards the Staff Only door. The two of them went through and up to the office.

'How's work over at the Dog going, Bob?' said Harry sitting at his desk. Bob did the same at his desk opposite.

'Good, Harry. The guys have worked their bollocks off. I reckon they'll have it finished end of next week.'

The door to the office opened and Louise walked in, loaded with shopping bags under each arm.

'All right, love, what you doing here?'

'Oh, the bloody car wouldn't start. I got the AA out but they couldn't get it going. They took it up the Merc dealers,' she said, dumping the bags in a chair.

'Hello, Bob, you all right darlin'?'

'I'm good, Lou. You want me to get Tom to run you home?' he asked, pulling his mobile out of his pocket.

'Yes, please, honey. My feet are killing me,' she said, slumping into a chair next to the shopping.

'You go home, love and put your feet up. I'll be home around ten,' said Harry, moving around the desk. He gave her a kiss on the cheek as Bob finished talking on the mobile.

'Tom's downstairs by the fire exit, Lou, the car's round the back. He'll run you home, ok?' said Bob, cracking a wide smile.

'Thanks. Right, I'll see you later, love. Don't work too hard,' she said, picking up her shopping bags and disappearing down the stairs.

'When's Pete back at work?' said Harry, walking over to the office window.

'Denis reckons he'll be right for opening night.'

'Good,' said Harry looking down at Louise climbing in the back of the Bentley. He watched Tom shut the door and get in the driver's side. He felt the increase in air pressure before he saw the blast. The building shook and the windows blew in with such force it threw him backwards into the middle of the room. He lay there winded and dazed, his face peppered with shards of glass. A few seconds later, like being hit with an electric shock, his mind caught up with the surrounding events.

'Lou!' he screamed, shaking off the shards of glass as he stumbled to his feet.

'Louise!' he screamed again. Reaching the glassless window, he stared down trying to see through the plumes of black acrid smoke.

Turning, he ran down the stairs, closely followed by Bob. His feet skidded as he shouldered the fire doors, bursting into the alley down the side of the club. He stood and stared, his face gaunt in horror and disbelief. The Bentley was bent and twisted out of shape; the passenger section engulfed in a ferocious ball of flame. Harry tried to move forward in a futile effort to save Louise, but Bob held him back as he continued to yell and scream her name. As Bob held him his eyes were drawn to graffiti on the back of the fire escape doors, and a bright red square with a stencilled yellow star next to a yellow *V*. He continued to hold Harry, his blood boiling at the thought of Viktor Volkov, and the loss of Tom and Louise. Sirens echoed off the buildings, growing louder in their cacophonous approach. Harry fell still and silent, his face contorting in shock and dismay. It changed to gritted fury and the need for retribution.

'We tell the police nothing, Bob. I want to find that fucker and kill him personally.'

They stood in silence as the cars and noise and blue lights piled into the alley, while beams of blue streaked through the smoke like a laser light show.

TWENTY

DCI Nichola Swan had just put her jacket on and was on her way out at the end of her shift. She got within a few feet of the door when it flew open, making her jump. DC Jonathan Cripp entered in an excited state.

'Oh, good, you're still here.'

'Not for long, what's going on, Jon?' she said, waiting patiently for him to spit it out.

'We've got Harry Knight downstairs in an interview room. Someone just blew his wife and driver up with a car bomb.'

'Shit, this has got well out of hand. Who's interviewing?' said Swan still trying to get her head around it.

'Mike's in with Bob Angel but Derick's out on a call, so get your skates on and you're in,' said Cripp, opening the door for her.

'Thanks, Jon,' she replied, following him down the stairs.

She got a rough account of the details from a scene of crimes officer. It was too early to get ballistics on the car bomb, and it was unlikely there would be any forensic evidence on the burnt-out husk of a car. Taking a pause to gather her thoughts she entered the interview room. Harry sat subdued behind the table, his hands clasped tightly together in front of him, causing his knuckles to go white. His solicitor sat upright and ready by his side. Swan introduced herself once again, before setting the recording equipment and running through the interview formalities.

'Mr Knight, I know this is difficult and I'm very sorry for your loss.'

She paused out of habit. This would usually be the point where a grieving spouse would break down or jabber on with furious accusations or apologies for taking up police time, or at least something. But there was no reaction. Harry just sat there staring through her, his mind somewhere else.

'As your wife was only in the car because hers broke down, I think we can assume someone meant this for you. Do you have any idea who would want to do this to you?'

'No,' was all Harry said. His eyes flicked to meet hers, but his voice remained void of emotion.

'Does this have any connection to the incident at the Dog-n-Duck public house, the week before last?'

'No.'

Same response, same tone.

'Mr Knight, we know you went to Viktor Volkov's club, Silk & Lace, on the same night as the pub attack. We have CCTV footage of you entering the club, and calls from residents who say they heard what sounded like a gunshot,' said Swan, feeling the tension build across the table.

'Has the explosion in your car got anything to do with a turf war between you and Viktor Volkov?' she said, trying to get an answer or a reaction out of Harry.

'No,' said Harry, as before.

His solicitor stepped in as Harry sat back emotionless.

'I must protest. Mr Knight has just lost his wife and a good friend. He came here of his own free will and has answered your questions to the best of his knowledge. He doesn't know who has done this atrocious act and as he is not under arrest, we are leaving.'

Swan knew that was as much as they would get tonight. She offered her condolences again and terminated the interview.

Cripp was waiting for her when she got back upstairs.

'Well, don't keep me in suspense. How'd it go?'

'Not good, Jon, Knight's not giving anything away. But I get the horrible feeling it's not police justice he's after,' she said.

'What can we do?'

'There's not a lot we can do, other than keep tabs on Knight and Volkov, and hope forensics find something on the car,' she said, pulling her jacket on for the second time that night.

'I don't hold much hope of that happening. Have a good night.'

'Thanks, I'll see you tomorrow.'

Cripp watched her go then reached for his phone.

TWENTY ONE

Bob met Harry outside the station. Harry thanked his solicitor warmly, his face turning grimly dark the moment he'd gone.

'They know about our trouble with Volkov,' said Bob.

'I know. We've gotta get this done tonight, before the coppers get all over it.'

They walked down the road and got into one of the waiting Range Rovers.

'You got the cars and the boys ready?' said Harry to Phil in front, his voice cold and determined.

'Yes, Boss, all set,' said Phil, in much the same mood as Harry.

'You got what I asked for, Bob?' Harry growled.

'Yes, Boss. No serials, untraceable.'

'Thanks, I owe you for this.'

'You don't owe me nothing, Boss. This is for Lou and Tom,' said Bob as they moved off into London traffic.
***

In the office above Silk & Lace, Viktor sat drinking with Ivan and Dimitri. They cheered as a newsflash announced two dead in a car bomb outside a London nightclub.

'Haha, fuck you, Harry Knight. Nostrovia,' yelled Viktor, raising his glass and laughing at the TV.

'The Irish didn't go cheap on the Semtex, da,' said Ivan, shaking his glass for a refill.

'This will draw a lot of heat. The police will be looking at everything we do,' said Dimitri with concern.

'Fuck them, you worry too much,' said Viktor busily shaking a line of coke onto his desk, before snorting it through a rolled up fifty.

'I still want to kill the other one,' said Ivan. The tape was off his nose but it was still purplish, and his eyes were still black in the corners.

'You will, Ivan, you will. We will find him and you can do whatever you want to him,' Viktor said, rubbing the powder off his nose.

'You should let things quieten down, Viktor.'

'Fuck off, Dimitri, you're spoiling my celebration. Fuck it, I'm off home,' he said, stumbling as he got up.

'You want me to get one of the men to take you?' asked Ivan.

'What, you think I fucking need babysitting? I drive myself,' he said, heading unsteadily out of the door. Ivan just laughed and waved him off before getting up himself.

'I'm off too. Lighten up, Dimitri. You need to relax.'

Dimitri watched him go. He hovered over the phone on the desk; he wanted to call Yuri and tell him about Viktor's reckless behaviour. His hand shook as he thought about it and only pulled back when he thought about what Viktor might do if he found out. The mobile went off in his pocket, making him jump.

'Yes,' he answered.

'It's me. Harry Knight's still alive. The bomb got his wife and driver instead.'

'Fuck, where is he now?' said Dimitri, his mind racing.

'No idea, but if I'd just killed Harry Knight's wife, I'd wanna be keeping my wits about me.'

'Ok, thanks.'

Dimitri hung up and rushed over to the window, just in time to see Viktor's Ferrari scream past the front of the club.

Shit.

***

The noise of the red Ferrari echoed off the buildings as it went past. Seconds later the light of a mobile phone exposed a face in ghostly luminescence as it made a call. Less than thirty seconds later it went off, enveloping him into the shadows once more.

***

Viktor drifted over the centre line, the rumble of tyres over the cat's eyes momentarily snapping him out of his cocaine and vodka haze. Fumbling with his phone he called Ana at his apartment, weaving dangerously along the road as he talked.

'Hey bitch, put something sexy on. I'll be home in a minute. YOU HEAR ME?' he shouted when she took too long to answer.

'Yes, Viktor, I'll see you in a minute.'

Throwing the mobile on the seat, Viktor cornered hard, turning off the main road towards his apartment block. A few hundred metres up the road he could see the back of a Range Rover, its brake lights burning bright. Beside it, facing him, the headlights of a large car on full beam hurt his eyes. The driver's door was open and two figures stood arguing. Arms were flapping in angry gestures silhouetted in the headlights.

'Arr, what the fuck is dis?' Viktor growled, banging his palms on the steering wheel as he slowed to a stop. Viktor hammered on the horn, causing one of the guys to turn and stick his finger up.

Motherfucker.

He was horny as hell and wanted to get back to the apartment and Ana. He resisted the urge to get his gun out of the glove box and scare the shit out of these guys. Instead, he decided to back up and go down a side turning and around them. Putting it in reverse he swung his head to look out the back at the same time as a black 4x4 drew up close behind him.

Ah for fuck's sake.

Viktor wound down the window, bashing on the horn as he stuck his head out.

'Move out the fucking way,' he yelled.

Out of the corner of his eye he caught some movement in the shadows. He stared as it came into view, his eyes growing wide in terror as he recognised what it was. Diving for the glove box, he scrambled to open it in the dark. The interior lit up as it fell open, allowing him to grab his gun. He never got to aim it. Harry emptied the whole magazine into Viktor's head and torso through the open window. The sound echoed and the barrel flash lit up the empty buildings on each side of the street in a macabre strobe effect. When it was over the silence was excruciating in its contrast. Harry stood and stared for a moment before walking calmly to the car behind. Bob stood by the driver's door with a small towel. As Harry passed him he placed the gun in the towel and climbed silently into the back. Bob wrapped the gun up, rubbing it as he did so, then climbed in, putting the towel on the passenger seat to get rid of later. He reversed, stopped and drove off down the side street. At the same time, the two cars in front drove slowly off in different directions. The red Ferrari's engine gurgled as it ticked over. Its headlights illuminated the deserted street as it waited for the pull away that would never come.

TWENTY TWO

The incident room was chaotic and noisy. DCI Nichola
Swan was busy updating the information boards. She
threw bullet points out to Cripp and the other detectives
as she read from the forensics report.

'No, nothing. All we've got is 13 empty shell casings.
No DNA, no fingerprints.'

'Anything around the vehicle?' said Detective Brooks.

'No, Gareth, nothing helpful. It's a busy cut-through:
there's a thousand bits of other people's crap all over the
road,' she said, writing under Harry's picture.

'What about Knight? Where was he at the time?' said
another detective, prompting Cripp to stand and answer.

'Mr Knight was at home all evening, grieving over his
wife. We have Bob Angel, his solicitor, and eight
employees who will swear he never left the house. He
even has the MP for Kensington North saying he

popped in to pay his respects around the time of Volkov's death,' said Cripp rolling his eyes to a groaning room.

'What about CCTV in the area? They must have got something,' said Brooks, still trying to stay positive.

'There's a suburban rat run of roads through the housing estates next to the shooting. No immediate cameras until the A3 on one side and the A100 on the other. We've been through hundreds of vehicle plates on both routes; none of them belong to Harry Knight. Also, CCTV in the St John's Wood area came up zero on any of Knight's cars leaving the area last night,' said Swan exasperated.

'Have we got any leads on the car bomb?'

'Forensics came back with Semtex in a magnetic container placed under the centre of the car. It was armed remotely by a mobile device and triggered by a mercury switch when the car moved off. It's a rare and sophisticated device so we're looking at the possibility of ex-military or para-military explosives experts.'

'Christ, this gets better and better. What about the mystery guy, Danny Pearson?' said Gareth.

'Dead end—his files are locked down tight. I don't know what he's done or who he worked for but he's got friends in high places. We've been told to back off and leave him alone,' said Swan, the frustration showing in her voice.

She looked at the room of blank faces.

'So. Any bright ideas, gentlemen?'

The room was a collective of shaking heads and silence.

***

Danny sat down at the kitchen table with his morning coffee. He flicked on the TV to the news channel. He half-watched a reporter going on about a politician who'd been caught cheating on his wife with a prostitute.

'Morning,' he said to Rob as he came in, clicking the kettle with a yawn.

'Eh, what, oh yeah, morning.'

His brother made him smile. He loved the normality of his life: get up, go to work, see Tina and cuddle up on the sofa with her, eat takeout, watch telly. For so long his life had been dirt, deserts and death, and after his wife and child died, just a hollow numbness. He chased the feelings away before they had time to drag his mood down and turned his attention to the next story on the news. The phone rang as he took in the headline: 'Two die in a car bombing in the capital last night'.

'I'll get it,' said Rob, heading for the hall.

Danny became transfixed by pictures of Knight's nightclub and the black charred remains of Harry's Bentley being taken away on the back of a police lorry. He fumbled to turn it up so he could hear the details, but they'd moved onto another story before he hit the volume button.

'Danny,' said Rob coming back in, his face as white as a sheet.

'Is it Harry? Did they kill Harry?' he asked, craving information.

'No, it's Auntie Lou. Someone killed Lou.'

Danny sat back stunned. He was about to make for the door to go to Harry's when the next report on the TV caught his attention: 'Russian-born London businessman, Viktor Volkov, shot dead in his Ferrari in a gangland-style shooting'.

Shit.

Danny borrowed his bewildered and upset brother's car and drove across to Harry's. After being let in through the gates, he was met at the door by Bob.

'Good of you to come, son. I don't know if Harry's up for visitors. I think May could do with some support, though,' said Bob softly. The atmosphere of loss covered the house like a blanket.

'What the hell happened, Bob?' asked Danny insistently.

Bob looked past him beyond the wall, before guiding him in and closing the door.

He took Danny to one side and spoke closely and quietly to him.

'Sorry, you can't be too careful. That bastard Russian tried to kill Harry with a car bomb. It was only because Lou's car broke down that she was in the Bentley. Harry's in bits, he blames himself for her death.'

'Jesus, what about Volkov and the shooting?'

'I can't talk about it. All you need to know is he got what he deserved,' said Bob with no show of emotion.

'No police comeback?'

'Let's just say this ain't our first rodeo, kid. Trust me—there's no police comeback,' said Bob with a hint of a smile.

Accepting what Bob said, Danny turned his thoughts to why he was there.

'Where's May?'

'Upstairs in her room. You know the way.'

He nodded to Bob and went up the stairs. He knocked lightly on May's door before entering. She was lying on her bed hugging a pillow. She turned to look at him with bloodshot teary eyes.

'Hi, Titch.'

She didn't say anything, just hugged him tight and buried her head in his chest as the tears flooded out. Sometime later Harry poked his head around the door; he looked dishevelled and tired. He acknowledged Danny with a wink and watched him console his daughter.

'Thanks, son,' he said softly before leaving the room.

TWENTY THREE

For the second time since Danny had returned home, he
stood by a grave at the City of London Cemetery. The
sun was shining this time, but the mood had never been
gloomier. Harry stood with his arm around May as she
wept. Danny stood on the other side with Rob and Tina
next to him. When the service was over the guests
gradually filtered off. Conversation was short and
awkward—other than condolences what was there to
say? May hugged Danny before wandering off with Bob.
Danny started to leave then turned to Harry.

'He got what he deserved. I would have done the
same.'

Nothing else was said. The two men shared a look and
exchanged a nod that said it all.

TWENTY FOUR

At the cargo terminal of Moscow's Domodedovo airport, a black limousine sat next to a hearse on the black expanse of tarmac. A huge cargo plane taxied slowly into its bay, guided to a stop beside them by the paddles of a fluorescent-jacketed airport official. Yuri Volkov stood perfectly still in the cold Moscow air, patiently waiting beside the limousine with no emotion showing. An orange hazard light spun on the back of the plane, and the massive rear cargo door opened slowly downwards on huge hydraulic arms. It clanged on the floor to form a ramp for unloading. Dimitri appeared at the top. He shook the pilot's hand before descending the ramp towards Yuri. They hugged briefly. Yuri kissed him on the cheek.

'I am sorry, Cousin,' Dimitri said with a mixture of remorse and a little fear.

'Is not your fault, Cousin. My brother was a fool. He brought this on himself.'

Dimitri gave a small relieved nod before taking his place beside Yuri as they waited. They watched four airport workers disappear into the cavernous plane, reappearing moments later with Viktor's coffin balanced on a pallet trolley. They placed it beside the hearse where the undertakers picked it up and slid it in the back. Yuri and Dimitri got in the back of the limousine and the two cars moved off towards the exit gate.

'When is the funeral?'

'Tomorrow,' said Yuri coldly.

'So soon?'

'What else could I do? Papa is so distraught I can barely console him. Is bad enough we cannot have an open coffin so people can see him to pay their respects. But for a father not to be able to see his son one last time…' Yuri said, his voice showing the first hints of anger.

'Surely Papa could see him before he's buried?'

'How, he has no fucking face you idiot,' growled Yuri, his eyes burning furiously.

'Yes, of course, sorry Yuri. What will you do about London?' said Dimitri, quickly trying to change the subject.

'Now we grieve. Tomorrow we bury Viktor. Papa is throwing a wake tomorrow night: a salute to Viktor's memory. When it is done, we talk about London.'

Yuri looked away making it very clear the conversation was over. They drove in silence the rest of the way, finally turning in and waiting for his armed security to open the gates to the Volkov family estate. The cars moved along the long shingle drive towards the eighteenth-century mansion. The building was huge with pillars either side of the door. Over thirty windows spanned its three-storey frontage. In the centre, just under the roofs' apex, sat the centuries old Volkov family crest. They moved to the entrance as the tall front doors opened. Filling the space was a huge mountain of a man, his crisp black suit visibly straining as he flexed. He stood aside to let them in, his blind eye shining below three claw-shaped scars that drew back through his blonde crew cut hair.

'How is Papa, Adrik?' said Yuri, turning to watch the undertakers bringing the coffin in.

'He's not good, Yuri. He's screaming for revenge and has drunk another bottle of vodka. He nearly shot me with that bloody antique shotgun of his.'

'Ok, ok, I'll go and talk to him. Tell them to put Viktor in the sitting room,' said Yuri, still keeping his emotions in check.

'Papa,' Yuri shouted as he made his way to his father's study.

'Yuri, is he here? Is Viktor home?' said Sebastian Volkov, his voice distressed and slightly slurred.

'Yes, he's here, Papa.'

Yuri walked in to find his father sitting behind his desk staring at him with bloodshot, teary eyes, an empty vodka bottle in one hand and an antique shotgun in the other.

'Come, Papa, give me the gun before you hurt someone. Remember what happened to Uncle Vlad.'

'That bastard deserved to get shot, he insulted your mother,' spat the old man, finally releasing his grip on the gun.

'Ok, ok. Let me get you some coffee and something to eat. You need to keep your strength up.'

'What I need is retribution. I want the man who did this to suffer. I want his family to suffer. I want him to wish he was dead. Then I want his head on my desk so I can spit in his eye.'

'He will, Papa, I swear it. As soon as we give Viktor his send off, he will,' said Yuri, putting his arm around his father's shoulder and leading him off towards the kitchen to sober him up.

'You are a good boy, Yuri. If you'd have been there this would never have happened,' the old man said, tears welling up in his eyes.

After plying him with coffee and food, Yuri took him up to his room and put him to bed. He returned downstairs to the sitting room where Dimitri and Adrik stood by Viktor's coffin. Yuri went to the drinks cabinet and poured three shots of vodka. He passed one to Adrik and one to Dimitri. With the nod of the head all three raised their glass.

'To Viktor,' they all said in salute, before knocking the drink back.

Yuri walked forward, placing his hand on the coffin lid.

'Adrik, when the wake is over you will return with me. I want Karl and Belek to come as well.'

When Yuri turned, the big man nodded and then left the room with Dimitri. They left Yuri alone with his thoughts and his brother.

TWENTY FIVE

Danny climbed the stairs up to Paul's Islington office. They'd cleared the boxes and Trisha Fields sat with a welcoming smile at a newly placed reception desk.

'Mr Pearson, nice to see you again,' she said cheerfully.

'Please, just call me Danny. Is he in?'

'Yes, he is, come on through' came a shout from the back office.

Paul's office had also been transformed. It looked neat and business-like and ready for action.

'Just the man I want to see. Take a seat,' said Paul, sliding a box file back on the shelf.

'Hello. That sounds ominous,' replied Danny, plonking himself in a chair.

'Firstly, sorry to hear about your mother. Are you holding up ok?' said Paul, genuine concern written over his face.

'I'm good, Paul. Now what did you want to see me about?' said Danny smiling but moving the conversation on, avoiding the personal topic of conversation.

'Er, fine, good. Ok, I've got four weeks' work with a security detail as team leader. The client is the UK's parliamentary commission for climate change. You'll be attending seminars in Minsk, Moscow, and Kiev. It's easy work, good money and good hotels.'

'Sounds good to me. When does it start?' asked Danny, perking up at the thought of something to get his teeth into.

'Eh, let me see. You'll fly out the fifteenth of next month. I've got ten guys in mind for the team, but I'd like you to check their files and choose which six you want to take.'

Paul turned around and pulled a different box file off the shelf, handing it to Danny.

'Thanks, Paul, I really appreciate this.'

'Don't thank me. I told you, men with your experience are hard to find. You're doing me a favour. This is a very important client. If this goes well I'll be expecting a lot more work from them.'

'In that case I'll read through this lot and let you know who I think is best,' said Danny noticing an apprehension in Paul's body language. He sensed there was something else on Paul's mind.

'Just spit it out, Paul,' he said with a grin.

'I never could get anything past you. Ok, certain important people have been bending my ear. They're not happy about car bombs and mob killings in London. They have mentioned your uncle's name more than once, and a certain DCI in the Met has been taking a big interest in you. She's been knocking on doors trying to get access to your classified files. I'll only ask you this once: are you involved in anything I should be worried about?'

Pauls eyes bore into Danny as he waited for an answer.

'I won't insult you by lying. We both know what happened. But I wasn't there when my aunt died and I wasn't there when Viktor Volkov was murdered. Harry finished it and is quietly grieving the loss of his wife,' said Danny openly, as he knew he could be with Paul.

'Excellent. Then no more need be said. Don't worry about DCI Nichola Swan. If she so much as breathes in your direction, she'll be directing traffic for the foreseeable future,' said Paul getting up to shake Danny's hand, signalling that the conversation was over.

'Send me a copy of your passport and I'll get all the travel and hotel arrangements booked,' he said waving him off and returning to his desk.

Danny left, saying goodbye to Trisha as he went.

TWENTY SIX

The funeral procession followed behind Viktor's hearse as it crossed the Moskva river. It passed the old 1950s Luzhniki Stadium before turning right into Moscow's Novodevichy Cemetery. The line of limousines and cars stretched so far back it took over five minutes to get them all in through the cemetery arch. They crowded around the centuries old Volkov family plot. It took up a large corner of the cemetery and was covered with a towering marble headstone, and was topped with strong, proud carvings of the Volkov family through the decades. The present head of the family, Sebastian Volkov, stood tall and as strong as his frail body would let him. His ice-blue eyes burned angrily and his face was tense. Yuri stood on his right, mirroring his father's show of strength as Viktor's coffin was placed in the ground. Sebastian stepped forward with Yuri still by his side.

'They will pay, my son. Pain, suffering and death is coming for them. This I swear,' he announced loudly for everyone to hear.

When he turned away Yuri stepped up and looked into the grave.

'Rest now, little brother. Even in death I'm clearing up your mess,' muttered Yuri before returning to his father's side.

The crowd of relatives, Mafia and associates moved slowly past Sebastian and Yuri, paying their respects. They moved off to their cars and waited to follow the head of the family back to the Volkov family mansion for the wake.

***

The wake followed the family tradition of food and drink and stories of past conquests; the power and brutality of the Volkov family's rule stretched across Russia. The old man was in his element, surrounded by old friends who, in their day, ran a network of corruption with an iron fist. Yuri walked around the guests as the new boss of the family business. They treated him with reserved respect as they greeted him. This suited Yuri fine; he'd never been the emotional type. He didn't need friends, he needed and wanted fear, respect and obedience. He spoke quietly in Adrik's ear before leaving him and moving to the empty library room. A few minutes later Adrik entered with Dimitri,

Belek and Karl. They fanned out and stood waiting for Yuri to speak.

'You have booked us a jet, Dimitri?'

'Yes, Yuri, 10:00am Tuesday.'

'Good, we will avenge my brother's death, but we mustn't take anything for granted. Viktor foolishly underestimated Harry Knight and got himself killed. We will not make the same mistake,' said Yuri, locking eyes with every one of them in turn. Dimitri nervously broke eye contact, making Yuri focus on him longer.

'Now go eat, drink and enjoy the hospitality,' he finally said, turning his attention away from Dimitri.

TWENTY SEVEN

'Whoa, there he goes again,' said Rob, shielding his eyes from the sun as he watched the golf ball sail off into the trees.

'Nice slice, old boy. Are you sure you're using the right end of the club?' said Scott, chuckling with Rob behind Danny.

'Yeah, yeah. Laugh it up, you couple of clowns,' said Danny sharing the good humour.

After Rob and Scott teed off straight down the fairway, Rob drove the golf cart up towards the green while Scott walked towards the rough with Danny.

'I'm sure you've realised by now golf isn't really my thing, Scotty boy, but thanks, mate, it was a great idea. Just what we needed, mate.'

'My pleasure, old man, although after that performance I don't think they'll let me back in the club again,' said Scott, dropping a golf ball out of his pocket into the long grass.

'Ah, there's a stock of luck. I've found your ball. Be a good chap and try to get this one near the sticky thing with a flag on it.'

'You can't keep popping balls out of your pocket every time I lose one, Scott.'

'I can if we want to get to the bar before they stop serving lunch,' said Scott, wandering off towards his own ball.

'Point taken. FORE!' he shouted as he ploughed the ball out of the rough.

An hour later they sat laughing and joking like old times in the clubhouse bar. The waitress brought out three meals and smiled politely at Scott's best attempts at chatting her up.

'Crashed and burned there, mate. Which reminds me, what's happening with you and Emma? Any sign of getting back together?' asked Danny, nodding to the barman for another round of drinks.

'I think the point of no return has long since passed, old boy. She's filed for divorce and has a very expensive solicitor who, ironically, is being paid for with my money. He's doing a superb job of ripping apart my finances and relieving me of my house,' said Scott with a shrug and a slight smile.

'You seem remarkably ok with that,' said Rob.

'Well, she's entitled to something, isn't she?'

'Scott, what aren't you telling us?' asked Danny, sensing Scott was holding back.

'Let's just say her solicitor isn't as good as mine and I've just signed a massive deal with a number of banks for upgrading their security software,' said Scott, raising his pint with a 'cheers'.

'Just like you to fall in shit and come out smelling of roses. Cheers,' said Danny, raising his pint with Rob in return.

'Every dog has his day my friend. Your day will come.'

Danny just smiled in return. He wasn't sure he'd ever find true happiness, or allow anyone to get that close to him again.

TWENTY EIGHT

The doorman watched the smart-suited man as he walked past the queue of people behind the roped-off entrance. Heads turned as he approached. An air of confidence and power emanated off him.

Oh great, what the fuck have we got here then? thought the doorman.

'Whoa. Sir, you'll have to wait in the queue like everyone else,' he said, putting his hand up to stop him. He was about to get more forceful when three more men moved up to join the man, the last of whom was the largest, scariest man he'd ever seen. His cloudy blind eye stared eerily below three deep grooved scars dragging back through his hair.

'Is there a problem, Yuri?' said Adrik leaning in slightly as he spoke. His deep, thick Russian accent rumbled in his chest.

'Yuri… Volkov. Err, sorry, Mr Volkov, I didn't know you were coming. Please come in.'

The doorman opened the door quickly for Yuri. He cowered behind it as Adrik and the others came past, a cold, hard look of contempt on their faces. Dimitri turned up and came in behind them. He spoke in the doorman's ear as he passed.

'Let everyone know Yuri Volkov is here. Tell them to do their jobs and keep out of his way,' he said nervously.

'DIMITRI, come here. I need to see the office,' said Yuri, his voice emotionless but raised slightly in annoyance.

'Sorry, coming Yuri,' said Dimitri scuttling off to lead the group upstairs.

As they went up, they met Ivan on his way down.

'Yuri, Adrik, is good to see you,' said Ivan, embracing each man in turn.

'Is good to see you, too, Ivan. I have some things to attend to now. When I'm done, I need to speak with you,' said Yuri, telling Ivan rather than asking him.

'Of course,' said Ivan with an acknowledging nod.

In the office Yuri sat behind the desk in Viktor's leather chair. Adrik sat down, filling the sofa, while Karl and Belek took the two armchairs. The tight-knit group fell silent, all eyes falling on Dimitri. They hung there for an excruciatingly long time, causing Dimitri to tremble slightly.

'Would you like me to get some drinks sent up from the bar?' said Dimitri trying to lighten the mood.

'No,' said Yuri bluntly.

'Get me everything you have on my brother's business setup—people, places and money. Everything, Cousin. NOW.'

'Yes, Yuri.'

Dimitri disappeared out the door as fast as he could without physically running. He was starting to think Viktor wasn't so bad after all.

'Karl, Belek, I want you two to find out everything about Harry Knight, his money, his businesses and his family. But be discreet, da?'

'Da,' said Karl.

Belek just got up and nodded. The two swiftly left, chatting loudly in Russian as they descended the stairs.

'Adrik, go and introduce yourself to the staff, let them know who is in charge, and get rid of that idiot doorman.'

Adrik got up and straightened his suit jacket before going down to the club. Once alone Yuri sighed and sat back in his seat. He pulled out his phone and dialled a number.

'Papa, I'm here. Yes, I will keep you informed. When it is done I will bring you his head, I promise. Now please get some rest.'

Yuri threw the phone on the desk and slid the desk drawers open, finding Viktor's gun and a bottle of vodka in the top one. He turned the gun over in his hand before picking the bottle up and dropping it in the bin. Under the bottle was a little bag of cocaine and a dust-covered mirror Viktor had for his personal use. Yuri looked at it in disgust before slamming the drawer shut.

Viktor was a fool.

TWENTY NINE

Harry pushed through the new doors to enter the Dog-n-Duck. It had been a week since his grand relaunch, and he was pleased to see the place was busy with early evening dinners. A few of the regulars he'd known for years offered their condolences. He gave them a courteous 'thank you' and made his way to the bar.

'All right, Denis, good crowd in?' said Harry to his bar manager.

'Yes, Harry, it's been packed since we opened.'

'That's what I like to see. Where's Pete, in the office?' he asked, moving towards the private door.

'Yeah, he's in there.'

Harry went out back and found Pete going through drinks orders, his plastered ankle sticking out straight, with his crutches propped in the corner.

'Hi Pete, how's the leg, son?'

'Itches like crazy, Harry. The cast comes off next week and I can't bloody wait,' said Pete, handing Harry a spreadsheet.

'Take a look at that. Takings are up thirty-five percent since the refurb. Customers love the new look and the chef's new menu's going down a treat.'

'That's great. I want you to know I appreciate all the hard work you and Denis have put in, Pete. I know I haven't been around much since Louise—,' said Harry, tailing off as he spoke.

'Don't mention it; it's the least we could do.'

Harry was about to say something when his phone rang. He signalled one minute to Pete then took the call.

'Phil.'

'Hi, Harry. I've just dropped the stuff from the cash and carry off at the club. Did you still want me to pick May up from college?' said Phil, leaving the club via the rear doors. The scorched, melted patch of tarmac where the car bomb had gone off made him shiver.

'Yes, please, Phil. Take her home and tell her I'll be back around six.'

'Ok, Boss,' said Phil hanging up and driving off towards Camden.

Fifty metres back Karl pulled out into traffic and followed at a discreet distance. It took forty minutes in the slow stop-start London traffic before Phil finally pulled up outside the college. He looked at his watch and wandered off down the street. Further back, parked on the other side of the road sat Karl. He took pictures of the car and Phil on his phone, then sat back waiting patiently as Phil disappeared out of view. A few minutes later he was back, a Greggs coffee in one hand and a doughnut in the other. Karl continued to watch him while he drank and ate. About fifteen minutes passed before a group of girls came out of the college doors. They chatted and hugged. Waving, May Knight peeled away from the others and got into the car. Karl made a note of the time and took more photos before carefully continuing to follow them. When the car eventually turned in through the electric gates of the Knight's home, Karl drove casually past and headed back towards South London and the Silk & Lace nightclub.

THIRTY

Dimitri had summoned Trevor Bailey and Lenard Timms to Silk & Lace. They entered the club full of attitude and false bravado. Bailey was back to his cocky self after having the cast taken off his wrist. Their faces fell as they walked through the foyer doors to the sight of Adrik beating one of the dealers to a pulp. He dropped the guy on the floor and stood staring at the two menacingly, blood dripping off the knuckle duster on his fist. Moving up to each side of Adrik stood Belek and Karl, glaring at them. Bailey and Timms stood frozen to the spot, fear creeping over them. They heard footsteps over the whimpering of the man on the floor. They got louder until Yuri appeared walking slowly around his men.

'Belek, show this piece of shit out,' said Yuri, never taking his eyes off Bailey and Timms.

Belek gave the semi-conscious man a bone-crunching kick to the ribs before grabbing the collar of his jacket and dragging him off through the kitchen to the back door.

'Sit,' ordered Yuri, the three of them moving around, forcing Bailey and Timms to sit in one of the round booths.

'You lost my merchandise and my money.'

'Yeah, but Viktor said we could make it up,' said Trevor, interrupting Yuri.

'I AM NOT MY BROTHER! You interrupt me again and it will be the last thing you do!' shouted Yuri, slamming his palms down on the table in front of them.

The terrifying figure of Adrik moved in close beside him. Bailey immediately shut up and the two of them shrank back in the booth as far as they could go.

'You know your way around the city. YES?'

They both nodded back to Yuri eagerly.

'I have a job for you. Do it and you will clear your debt. Now go with Belek and Karl, they will tell you what to do,' said Yuri, turning and leaving with Adrik. The meeting was over.

Belek beckoned them over as Karl rejoined them from the kitchen.

'Come, come we go,' he said.

Shaking with the knowledge they'd narrowly escaped a beating—or worse—Bailey and Timms looked at each other and slid out of the booth. A knot grew in Bailey's stomach as he followed the menacing Russian pair out of the club.

What the hell have I gotten myself into now?

THIRTY ONE

They came out of Harry's betting shop and climbed in the back of the Range Rover.

'Drop me and Bob at the club please, Phil, I've gotta do the VAT return. If you can pick May up from college and drop her home, you'd be doing me a big favour.'

'No problem, Boss.'

'Good lad. The Johnson twins are keeping guard at mine, so drop May and get off home. I'll see you in the morning.'

'Ok, thanks.'

After he dropped them off, Phil checked his watch. With plenty of time to spare he took a slow drive across North London towards May's college. He got within a couple of miles when a red BMW cut in front of him from a side road.

'Fucking idiot,' he said out loud, thumping the horn. He'd driven behind it a few hundred metres, when the car slammed on its brakes. Phil jumped on his, just managing to stop short of the car. He was about to breathe a sigh of relief when a white Transit van hit him from behind.

'Oh, for fuck's sake,' he said, getting out.

He got near the back and looked up from his broken taillight to the Transit. It took a second for him to register the sight of two wide-eyed men in ski masks staring back at him.

Oh shit, gotta get out of here.

He was just turning to get back in the car when his arms were grabbed from behind. He felt the zip ties tighten and cut into his wrists. He tried to twist to see who held him. A thick clear plastic bag was pulled tightly over his head and zip-tied around his neck. Through his claustrophobic panic Phil saw the distorted vision of two men in ski masks stepping in front of him. One turned and hit him hard in the stomach. Phil went down on his knees. The wind knocked out of him, puffing the bag up. His immediate reflex was to gasp air back in, but the bag sucked tight over his face causing his lungs to burn and blind panic to set in. The men had got back in the Transit and it reversed down the street fast. Screeching to a halt, it then sped off down a side street, leaving Phil alone thrashing around on the floor with his arms secured behind him. He tried desperately to rip a hole in the bag on the rough tarmac. The blood vessels in his eyes started to rupture and his head was spinning. He was aware of a woman grabbing him and pulling frantically at the plastic.

'Someone help, please. I can't rip it,' she screamed out in distress.

Everything was going dark. He convulsed as his body went into shock.

'Let me try,' came a man's voice. 'It's too thick. I need something sharp. Has anyone got a knife or scissors? Quick—we're losing him,' he bellowed.

Phil's movements slowed to a stop and his eyes went dull and lifeless. The man managed to punch a small hole through the tough plastic with his car keys. By the time he got it ripped enough to try mouth-to-mouth it was too late.

THIRTY TWO

May came out of the college with her friends like any other day. She looked for Phil on the road but couldn't see him. When she got near the kerb, the side door of a white Transit van slid open and two big men in ski masks burst out. One wrapped his arm around May's neck, dragging her backwards into the back. The other man was armed with a crowbar and floored two of her friends with a powerful swing. He jumped back in, sliding the door shut behind him. The engine screamed and the van sped off down the road in a cloud of diesel smoke. Everyone was still in the shock of the moment. A few were on their phones to the police while others helped May's floored friends. Two boys stood on the college steps videoing the abduction on their phones; they filmed the van as it disappeared from view.

***

Belek twisted May's arm painfully back as Karl held her tight.

'Hold her still, Karl,' he said, pulling her jumper sleeve up over her elbow and twisting it tight on her arm. He pulled a syringe out of his pocket and injected it into her vein. Her muffled screams died to a soft murmur as the heroin high washed over her.

'Ok, go, go. Drive to the whorehouse,' said Belek to Trevor and Lenard in the cab.

Trevor looked at Lenard nervously. Selling drug baggies to the party crowds and losers of London was one thing; murder and kidnapping young women off the streets was something else altogether.

'You boys like the plastic bag trick, yes?' said Karl to Bailey and Timms.

They nodded their approval out of fear, then sat rigidly looking where they were going, just hoping Karl and Belek would forget they were there.

'One thing's for sure, it wasn't environmentally friendly for him, eh,' said Belek, laughing and slapping Karl on the back.

'We're here,' said Bailey from the front.

'Then go clear the way, idiot, so we can bring her in,' said Belek with contempt in his voice.

Bailey had none of his usual cocky comments. He got out of the van and pressed the intercom buzzer on the door.

'Yes.'

'It's Trevor, I've got the delivery for you,' said Bailey, looking up and down the street anxiously.

'Bring it in, we are ready,' said a woman's voice as the lock buzzed. Bailey signalled to Timms and a second later the side door of the van slid open. Belek and Karl brought May in through the door, propping her up either side. From a distance she looked like a young woman being helped home by two friends after a few too many drinks. Once inside Belek threw her over his shoulder and thumped up the stairs to the first floor of the large Georgian three-storey townhouse. They were met on the landing by the madam of the house, Magda Galewski.

'Where?' grunted Belek.

'Top floor, the door on the left. Ana will look after her.'

Belek shifted May on his shoulder and marched up the stairs, followed by Karl. Trevor stayed with Magda.

'I don't like this,' said Magda, her Polish accent coming across cold and hard.

'I'm not fucking chuffed about it myself. If you want to take it up with Yuri, be my guest,' he said, some of his attitude returning. Magda just glared and returned to her reception desk. Behind her three of the working girls sat on a collection of large sofas. Anywhere else three men carrying a spaced-out girl over their shoulder would raise the alarm, but here among the kink and sleaze and perversions it didn't even raise an eyebrow. A couple of minutes later, Belek and Karl came back down the stairs.

'Make sure she's looked after until we return,' said Belek not waiting for a response before descending the stairs.

'You, Shithead, you can drop us off then fuck off. We will call you when we need you.'

'Where do you want dropping off, the club?'

'No, drop us off at Viktor's apartment. We keep clear of the club until this is over.'

Trevor gave Magda a look before following the other two out of the building.

THIRTY THREE

As evening rolled in Danny sat round Scott's talking about old times.

'I saw Arnie Swinton the other day,' said Scott, clearing away their Domino's Pizza boxes.

'No! The terminator from school, that guy used to beat the crap out of us. Where'd you see him?'

'You'll love this, old boy, he's working at Sainsbury's on the deli counter,' said Scott grinning.

'What, no way,' said Danny chuckling.

'And get this, he's now fat and bald with thick bottle glasses. I spent best part of ten minutes selecting items off the counter and then changing my mind. I think he would have punched me if his supervisor wasn't standing beside him.'

The two of them rolled up laughing as Danny's phone buzzed.

'Hello.'

'Danny, it's Harry. Sorry to bother you, son, but you haven't heard from May or Phil today have you?'

Danny immediately picked up on Harry's trepidation, sending a chill of foreboding down his spine.

'No, what's happened?' asked Danny so bluntly Harry stopped trying to sound unconcerned.

'Phil went to pick her up from college and I can't get hold of either of them; their phones just go to answerphone.'

'Have you heard anything from south of the river since Viktor?' said Danny, his mind already working overtime.

'No, nothing. Look, son, she's probably just got Phil to take her to a friend's and—what's that, Bob? The police are here,' said Harry going quiet as he talked to the police in the background.

'Harry, Harry, what's going on?' said Danny impatiently, trying to hear the voices away from the phone.

'I've got to go. Someone's grabbed May from college and Phil's dead. I'll call you later,' said Harry hanging up.

'What's up?' said Scott.

'Do you remember that big kit bag I asked you to look after? You know, the one I gave you when I sold the house after Sarah and Timmy died. Have you still got it?'

'Yes, it's in the loft. What's going on?' said Scott, his curiosity piqued.

'May's been taken and I've got a really bad feeling about it,' said Danny, already heading up the stairs to Scott's loft hatch.

'Anything I can do to help, old man?' asked Scott, concerned. He'd also known May since they were kids.

'I need you to drive me somewhere, mate,' shouted Danny from the landing.

'Eh ok, fine. What's in the bag?'

'Souvenirs, Scotty boy, souvenirs,' said Danny disappearing up the loft ladder. He emerged at the hatch a few seconds later and dropped a large green kit bag onto the landing with a thud.

THIRTY FOUR

'Pull up here, Scott,' said Danny when they were a hundred metres up the road from Silk & Lace.

'Right, all I want you to do is keep an eye on that door. Any excitement or dangerous-looking Russians turn up, tell me. Just talk normally into the throat mic and I'll hear you, ok?' said Danny, covering up his own throat mic in his baggy black hoodie.

'Roger that, old boy,' said Scott, excited with the cloak and dagger mission.

'Yeah ok, Scott, calm down, just talk normally. I'm just going for a look about, that's all.'

'Affirmative,' said Scott grinning.

'You arsehole,' chuckled Danny exiting the car.

He walked casually past the club with his hoodie up, his face shrouded in shadow. He noticed a new doorman at the entrance as he passed. Ducking in under an archway two buildings down, he walked around to a service bay at the back of the club. There were spaces for three cars, only one was filled with an old Ford Escort. The back of the club had a metal door which was open and led to the kitchens. The service area was brightly lit by a floodlight mounted on the black metal fire escape that ran up the back of the club. Danny waited in the shadows until a kitchen worker finished his cigarette and went inside. Noticing the CCTV camera above the door, he popped up on the bins and then the flat roof of the building next door. He kept to the far side until he got to the back of the building. With a short run up he leapt across onto the fire escape. Swinging over the banister he reached across and thumped the top of the floodlight hard. The sudden shock caused the white-hot filament to blow and darkness to consume the service bay. Swinging back onto the steps, he kept his feet light and climbed the fire escape towards the top floor. He froze momentarily as one of the lap dancers came out for a smoke. She stared into the dark at the floodlight, her large overcoat swinging open to display the lingerie underneath.

'Hey, Benny, tell Ivan that bloody light has gone again,' she said, shouting through the kitchen door. She stubbed the cigarette out with her stilettos and went back in. Danny climbed until he was next to the office window. After taking a few darting glances to check it was empty, he took his old commando knife out of its sheath and slid it up between the sash windows. Wiggling it he flicked the latch across and slid the window up.

'Everything still quiet out front, Scott?'

'Absolutely, old man, where are—'

'Just a yes or no please, Scott,' said Danny, smiling at Scott's rambling.

'Oh, right, yes of course.'

Danny moved across the office to the door and listened before opening it. He stepped forward and checked the stairs—all clear. He left the door slightly ajar so he could hear anyone coming and went to the desk. Looking through the paperwork on top, it was just bills, brewery orders and staff rotas. He checked the desk drawers finding the gun in the top one. Beside it was a little notebook. He thumbed through the pages of phone numbers and supplier details until he found a username and password for the CCTV system. Danny looked around the office until he spotted a DVR and screen on top of a filing cabinet.

'Scott, would you be able to remotely see a CCTV system?'

'With a little information, yes.'

'What do you need?'

'Eh, the make of DVR—that's the video recording unit to you—and the username and password would be handy,' said Scott in a hushed voice.

'The unit is a Trent2450DVR and I've got the username and password. You don't need to whisper, Scott, no one can hear you.'

'Oh, yes, right. Tap *Enter* on the keyboard and then log in with details you have.'

'Ok, got it, now what?'

'Click on *Users* and then *Create new.*'

'Yep.'

'Use something like 'service log' for username, that way they probably won't twig if someone looks through it. Just use 'password' for password, then I'll talk you through settings.'

While following Scott's instructions, Danny heard the door at the bottom of the stairs.

'Is that it, Scott? Gotta get going, mate,' said Danny, hearing footsteps and voices.

'Change the port forwarding to 8080 then save and exit,' said Scott hastily.

Danny hit the save button and watched an egg timer spin round on the screen. He could hear the noise from the stairs getting louder.

Come on, come on.

The door to the office opened just as the screen refreshed back onto the camera feeds. Ivan looked at it. The flicker had caught his eye as he entered. It looked like it always did, so he dismissed it. Luckily the distraction kept his eyes away from the sash window as it closed silently through its last centimetres.

THIRTY FIVE

When they got back to Scott's, Danny called Harry while Scott went to work on his computer.

'Harry, it's Danny.'

'No, son, it's Bob. Harry's still tied up with the police.'

'No news of May then,' said Danny, already knowing the answer.

'No, with Phil getting murdered there are more cops here than at Millwall on match day. All we want to do is get rid of them and find May, our way,' said Bob with an uncharacteristic crack in his voice.

'Hold it together, Bob. Let me know if you hear anything. I'll be over in the morning.'

'Ok, son, I'll tell Harry you called.'

The phone went dead and Danny returned to Scott.

'How are you getting on with the CCTV, Scotty boy?' asked Danny walking through to Scott's office.

'Already done, old boy. What are we looking for?'

'Not sure, maybe something, maybe nothing. I want to work through the days since Viktor Volkov died,' said Danny looking over Scott's shoulder at the camera feeds. 'So how do I do that?'

'Pull up a chair, you caveman, and I'll walk you through it,' said Scott, rolling his eyes.

A few hours later Scott put a beer down in front of him.

'How's it going?'

'Hmm, not much happening so far. This guy in the suit and the musclehead have been running things after Viktor's death. The police and DCI Swan have been in and out questioning staff,' said Danny, pointing at stills of Dimitri and Ivan.

'The suit guy's not been around for a while now.'

'Where are you up to now?' said Scott, yawning.

'Err, this is Wednesday the twelfth in the evening. Sorry, Scott, it's late. I'll go,' said Danny realising what the time was.

'No, no, you carry on, old boy. I'm off to bed. Just crash in the spare room when you're done.'

'Thanks, Scott.'

'Don't mention it,' shouted Scott from the hall as he walked off.

Swigging his beer, Danny trawled through more hours of CCTV recordings. He was just about to turn in when the arrival of Yuri and his entourage reignited his interest. The authority and fear created by the man was easy to see, even with no sound to the video. Things moved quite fast from then. He saw Belek and Karl leave. Then he saw the formidable Adrik with Ivan talking to the doorman. It got heated and Adrik destroyed the man with a frightening display of fighting skills you wouldn't expect from a man of his size. Afterwards, Adrik and Ivan dragged him out into the street and threw him in the road, kicking him unconscious before returning to the club laughing. Danny continued to watch the feeds, fast-forwarding and playing as people came and went, until he saw a nervous Trevor Bailey and Lenard Timms entering the club.

Hello. Ginger and his mate, interesting.

He watched some more, rubbing his eyes as tiredness set in. He was fast-forwarding through when a glimpse of a visitor caught his eye. He rewound and played.

Hmm, what are you doing there?

Finally, Yuri left with Adrik and Dimitri, leaving Ivan to run the place once more. Danny forwarded until the feeds were up to date, but there was no sign of them returning to Silk & Lace.

THIRTY SIX

May opened her eyes slowly. Her head was foggy and heavy and it took a while to find focus. The sight of the room was too confusing for her to take in. There was a large wooden X on the wall with shackles in each corner. A six-foot high stainless steel cage sat on the other side of the room. As clarity of thought started to return, the sight of the whips, floggers and sex objects on the wall opposite threw her into a panic. She bolted upright on the bed and lurched forward for the door, only to be wrenched backwards onto the floor. Coughing and gasping, she felt the leather collar around her neck and the chain leading from it to a metal ring in the wall.

'Help, please anyone, help!' she shouted.

The door opened almost immediately and Ana entered in a panic, her bra, knickers and stockings showing through the thin silk dressing gown. She totted over on ridiculously high stilettos.

'No, no, please be quiet or they will come,' she said, helping May back on the bed, her eyes wide and scared as she looked back over her shoulder at the door. 'That's better. Please be quiet. Are you thirsty? I'll get you a drink,' said Ana, grabbing a bottle of water by the bed. May drank, managing to compose herself a bit.

'What's happening to me? Where am I?'

'I'm sorry, I don't know. Yuri's men brought you here and told me to look after you.'

'Who are you?' said May, feeling the padlock on the back of the collar.

'Ana.'

'Ana, you've got to get me out of here, please,' said May pleading.

Ana's whole body shook as she nervously chewed her nails.

'I can't. I'm sorry, they will kill me. I'm so sorry, please, I'm sorry,' she said, tears welling up in her eyes, her head whipping round towards the door at the sound of footsteps on the stairs. The door burst open and Adrik entered, his cloudy blind eye and deep scars casting a vision of nightmares. Karl and Belek stepped out from his shadow and moved to one side as Yuri entered the room, cold and calm. He moved slowly towards her, picking a piece of lint off the arm of his immaculately tailored suit as he approached.

'Miss Knight, how lovely to make your acquaintance,' he said quietly, his eyes cold as ice.

'Let me out of here, you fucking prick,' spat May through gritted teeth.

'You leave us,' said Yuri, shooting a look at Ana.

She left, keeping her head down, too afraid to look at any of them.

The men all closed in around May. Belek pulled some gardening secateurs out of his pocket.

'I just need a little something from you,' said Yuri, the slightest hint of a smile flickering across his lips.

Ana, Magda and the girls in the reception looked pensively at each other as the screaming echoed down from the top floor.

***

Scott dropped Danny in St John's Wood the next morning. A police car and a tatty blue Mini sat outside Harry's house. He got Bob on the intercom at the gate and was buzzed through. He walked across the gravel past another police car and nodded to three of Harry's boys who were chatting to two officers. The front door opened and Bob greeted him.

'All right, son, Harry's in the lounge with plod and that DCI woman, Swan.'

'No news then?' said Danny noting the tired bags under Bob's eyes.

'No, nothing, and these clowns ain't helping either,' said Bob through gritted teeth.

Danny went through into the lounge to be greeted by male and female police officers and DCI Swan all looking in his direction. Harry sat in the middle of them looking tired and strained.

'Mr Freeman or should I say Mr Pearson, you do keep popping up in the most interesting places,' said Swan, a hint of sarcasm in her voice.

'DCI Swan, I could say the same thing about you,' replied Danny bluntly.

She frowned at his comment before discarding it and turning back to Harry.

'That's all for now, Mr Knight. I'll leave the two officers out front for the time being. If you hear or think of anything, ring me.'

Harry just nodded as the officers left. Danny followed Swan out to the door.

'Do you have any insight into May's disappearance, Mr Pearson?' she asked, stepping onto the drive.

'Who was the ginger guy threatening the woman on the riverbank the other week?'

'Did you want to make a statement?' asked Swan, frowning again.

'No, I just want to know who he is and where I can find him,' said Danny, his face serious and voice without humour.

'You know I can't tell you that,' she said, curiosity piqued.

'And you know I can't tell you about Louise Knight or Viktor Volkov's deaths. But we both know what happened, don't we?'

'What is it you want, Mr Pearson?' asked Swan, curiosity turning to impatience.

'Call me Danny.'

'What is it you want, Danny?'

'I want my cousin back and I believe new characters connected to Viktor Volkov are responsible for her abduction. I need to know where Ginger is and I don't have time to fuck about. You help me and I'll help you take down Volkov's operation.'

Swan paused trying to weigh up the risks, rewards and consequences of trusting Danny. It seemed like ages before she finally responded.

'Twenty-eight Highbury Flats, Kingston, and call me Nichola,' she said, handing him her card.

'Thank you,' said Danny taking her card, his eyes locking on hers.

'This is between us, just us. Don't make me regret telling you.'

Danny nodded before adding, 'They have one of yours on the payroll.'

'Who?'

'I need to be sure first, then I'll let you know.'

Swan didn't answer; she just turned and left.

THIRTY SEVEN

Danny turned and went back inside.

'What was all that about?' asked Bob from within.

'Just following possibilities, Bob. I'm not good at sitting around waiting for things to happen.'

'I know, son. This is killing all of us,' said Bob, looking over his shoulder at Harry.

'How's he holding up?'

'Not good. May's all he's got.'

The buzzing intercom from the gate interrupted them.

'Yes,' answered Bob, stabbing on the intercom button.

'I've got a package for Mr Knight.'

'Ok, coming.'

Danny went through to see Harry while Bob went to the gate.

'Harry.'

'Danny, you heard anything?' said Harry, a hopeful desperation in his voice.

'No, sorry, but I'd like to borrow a car. I've got a few things I need to check out.'

Bob interrupted them and handed Harry the jiffy bag package. He ripped the top off without paying it much attention and casually peered in to see what it was.

'Oh, Jesus, no, no,' said Harry slumping into the sofa, his hands trembling.

Danny and Bob both moved in to see a severed finger in the bag and a red card with a yellow star and a *V* on it. Harry suddenly stood bolt upright clenching and unclenching his fists.

'Get everyone, we're going to Silk & Lace. I'm going to kill all those fuckers and get May back,' he shouted with rage. Danny had to grab him to make him listen to him.

'She's not at the club. Harry, listen to me. I checked it out last night, she's not there,' he said staring at Harry, waiting for the information to sink in.

'She's not there,' said Harry slumping down for a second time.

'No, listen to me. OK?'

Danny looked at Harry and Bob silently looking back.

'Get plod in from outside and get DCI Swan back here, ok? Get them out there looking for May. I need to borrow a car. I've got to find one of Volkov's runners.'

'Me and some of the boys will come with you,' said Harry, anger and frustration returning to his voice.

'No, I need you here to tell me if anything else happens.'

Danny paused, his face like granite and eyes blazing.

'I'll be better off doing this alone. Trust me.'

'Give him the keys to the Merc, Bob,' said Harry. There was something different about Danny, dark and dangerous, like he'd been when they went to Silk & Lace. Bob got the keys and followed Danny out.

'What exactly did you do in the army?' he asked as Danny got into the car.

'I wasn't in the army, Bob. I was one of the people you called when the army needed help, that's as much as I can say. But I promise you this: I will find May and I will bring her home.'

***

South of the river, Ivan drove down a side road off the Elephant and Castle. He passed a collection of car workshops and storage units and a furniture maker's under the railway arches of London transport. He stopped at the last unit. It was plain and sign-less with a closed, rusty red metal shutter and solid metal door. He got out and looked around to make sure no one had followed him before banging on the shutters. The door made a metallic screech as the bolts drew back, then creaked as Adrik swung it open. Ivan stepped past him before swinging it shut again. The unit was dimly lit and full of boxed TVs and new electrical goods. Yuri sat in the middle drinking tea out of a polystyrene cup.

'Ivan, you drink this shit? God I hate this fucking country,' he said, turning his nose up at the cup and throwing it in the trash.

'No, I can't stand their British tea. You wanted to see me, Yuri.'

'I have some information for you, Ivan.'

'You found him?'

'Da, I have his name and the address of where he's living,' said Yuri pulling an envelope from his inside pocket.

'Thank you, Yuri. You are happy for me to kill him.'

'Da, painfully, I hope. There is an added bonus—he is Harry Knight's nephew. Take Karl with you when you go. Our informant tells me he has former military experience. I don't want any fuck-ups, you understand?' said Yuri, calm and unconcerned as usual.

'I understand.'

'Good. Karl is busy today. You do this tomorrow.'

'Yes, Yuri.'

Yuri stood and straightened his suit jacket before stepping out of the unit. Adrik grinned at Ivan, gesturing for him to leave. The meeting was over.

THIRTY EIGHT

Danny parked way down the road from Highbury Flats. Harry's fifty-thousand-pound Mercedes would stick out like a sore thumb next to the local authority flats. He walked up to the intercom by the entrance door and pressed the buttons for twenty-four.

'Hello,' came a female voice.

'Hi, sorry to bother you. I've got a parcel, but the address isn't clear. Is that Mrs—,' said Danny, leaving a lingering pause.

'Mrs Daniels.'

'Mrs Daniels, no I think it's something like Bailey,' he said.

'Oh, that'll be Amy or her son, Trevor, at number twenty-eight.'

'Thanks, love, sorry to bother you,' said Danny pressing number twenty-eight. He waited patiently until a woman's voice finally came over the speaker.

'Yeah.'

'Hi, I've got a parcel for Mrs Daniels.'

'You've got the wrong flat. This is twenty-eight—Mrs Bailey. You want number twenty-four.'

'Mrs Bailey, are you Trevor's mum?'

'Who's asking?' she said suspiciously.

'Sorry, it's Steve. I used to go to school with Trev,' said Danny.

'Oh, hi Steve. Sorry, Trevor's not here at the moment,' said Amy now at ease.

'No bother, Mrs Bailey. I haven't got time to stop, anyway. Just tell him I said hi.'

'Ok, bye,' she said as the intercom clicked off.

Steve's a common enough name. Trevor must have known enough Steves or Stevens at school to discount the message.

Danny passed the flats, spotting number twenty-eight on the corner of the second floor. He noticed the Red Lion pub opposite and entered, heading to the bar. The pub was old and tired with tatty paintwork and a threadbare carpet, and a noticeable lack of customers. He ordered a pint and a packet of crisps, took a seat by the window and waited. Waiting had been a staple skill in the SAS. More than once his team had hidden in ditches and dugouts, unable to move, pissing and shitting where they lay so they didn't give their position away. Just waiting and watching for a target for hours and hours. Waiting for Trevor with a pint and a packet of crisps was a relative luxury.

Just over an hour later, Trevor drove past with Lenard in the passenger seat of an old tuned-up, gurgling Ford Focus RS. They parked outside the flats opposite. Danny watched as they got out laughing and joking. Lenard wandered off, presumably towards his own house. Trevor tapped a code into the entrance lock and disappeared up the stairwell. A few seconds later he emerged along the second-floor walkway and entered the flat. Danny drained his drink and left. He moved the car up to a space in front of Trevor's and got out. Grabbing the tyre iron out of the boot he smashed Trevor's indicator light. The car immediately went into alarm, lights flashing and horn shrieking in short blasts. Walking over to the entrance door Danny pressed twenty-eight. Trevor's voice came over it after a few seconds.

'Yo, who dis?' he said in an annoying attempt at an American rapper.

'Yo, Trev, mate, your car alarm's goin' mental,' said Danny in his best copycat tone before walking off.

'Who's this? Hello, hello?'

Trevor came out a few seconds later, peering over the wall at his noisy car. He hurried along the walkway and emerged out of the entrance. He pressed the button on the key remote to shut the car up and noticed the broken glass from his indicator. He was bending down swearing when he saw feet standing behind him. He never got upright to see who they belonged to; Danny's blow from the tyre iron plunged him into dark unconsciousness.

***

Trevor came round sometime later into total panic. He was hog-tied, hands to feet zip-tied behind him, his head was covered in a hessian sack tied around his neck. He was bouncing around in a hard, small space he assumed was the boot of a car. The first thought through his thumping head was that Yuri had no use for him anymore and was going to kill him. Pulling at the ties in a futile attempt at freedom, Trevor started to shake uncontrollably with fear and dread. The car journey went on for what seemed like ages. It finally came to an abrupt stop, smacking Trevor's head into the back of the seat. He groaned as the car ticked over, the pain in the front of his head now matching the pain in the back. He could hear the sound of a metal shutter moving before the car moved again and then stopped. The engine shut off and the shutter sound followed. The boot opened and someone lifted Trevor out, dropping him to the ground in one swift movement.

'Please, Yuri, it wasn't me, it was Lenard. He was skimming money off the top. Please, you've got to believe me,' he said in a muffled voice, sobbing through the hood. A kick in his guts silenced him and he gasped to suck air in.

'It's not about tha,t you stupid fuck. Yuri wants to know who you told about the girl's location?'

'I ain't said nothin', I promise. I never—'

'You must have said something about where she is or who she is,' Danny stood shouting just inches above Trevor's head.

'I—I never told anyone about Magda or the whorehouse. It must have been Ana—she was looking after her. It must have been her.'

'Don't blame Ana, you spineless shit. The address, who did you tell about the address?'

'No one, I swear,' said Trevor, shaking profusely.

Danny pushed his finger hard into Trevor's temple causing him to freeze, too scared to breathe, a wet patch spreading across his crotch.

'Say the address. SAY IT. Then you swear to me you told no one or I'm going to blow your brains out.'

'No, no please, please, twenty-three Orchard Crescent, Bermondsey and I didn't tell anyone.'

'BANG,' shouted Danny down Trevor's ear, causing him to jerk violently.

He pulled the sack off Trevor's head and gave him a couple of light slaps on the cheek.

'Thank you, Ginge, you've been most helpful,' he said, grinning at Trevor staring back at him in disbelief.

'You fucking bas—'

Danny shoved a cloth in his mouth before he could say anymore and wound tape around his head to keep it in place.

'Right, listen up. You lay here and be quiet and I might not tell Harry Knight about you helping to kidnap his daughter. Nod if you understand,' said Danny holding Trevor by the throat. He nodded slowly.

'Good. You sit tight and I'll be back.'

Danny pulled the shutter door up and drove out before shutting it, leaving Trevor alone in the dark. He knocked on the door of the house and waited until it opened.

'You all done, old boy?' said Scott casually to Danny.

'Yeah, thanks Scott. I've got another favour to ask you,' said Danny with a look Scott knew from old as not to be messed with.

'Intriguing, yes of course. What is it?'

'Don't go in the garage before I get back.'

'Eh, yes I suppose. What on Earth have you put in there?' asked Scott, peering around at the garage door.

'Not something you want to get involved in, mate. Promise me you won't go in.'

'Ok, I promise.'

Danny cracked a big grin to his friend as he got back into the car.

'I owe you, Scotty. I'll be back as soon as I can.'

'You better be,' said Scott, waving him off before closing the door.

THIRTY NINE

Parked across the road in the shadows, Danny sat
watching the large three-storey Georgian townhouse. He
waited an hour as various men came and went, shuffling
off nervously into the night. The crescent itself was quiet
with hedges and trees lining either side of the road; they
also shielded the brothel from prying eyes. With no sign
of Yuri or his men, he crossed the street and pressed the
buzzer.

'Hello?' came Magda's voice over the speaker.

'Err, hello. I was told to come here if I wanted, err,
company,' said Danny acting nervously.

'Who told you?'

'Err, a skinny ginger guy, Trevor.'

'Ok, come in, up the stairs,' came Magda's voice as
the lock buzzed open.

The decor inside was modern and tasteful, which surprised Danny. He met Magda sitting behind her desk at the top. Behind her half a dozen prostitutes in lingerie and silk gowns sat around on red velvet sofas.

'Evening, gorgeous. This your first time?' Magda asked with a false smile. She handed him a leather folder like a menu in a restaurant.

'Tell the girls what you want, yeah? You pay first, ok, prices are all in there. Now what's your preference, white, black, Asian?'

'Trevor told me about a girl called Ana. He said she would look after me,' said Danny trying to sound insistent without commanding.

'Ana is busy, but Caprice here will look after you,' Magda said, summoning a leggy blonde woman from the sofa.

'No, no. Sorry, I want Ana. I'm happy to pay,' said Danny, pulling a roll of notes out of his pocket, courtesy of Trevor.

'Ok, ok. Caprice go and get Ana,' ordered Magda eyeing the money.

'Two hundred for Ana, you pay now. She's a very special girl.'

'I'm sure she is,' said Danny handing over the money as he eyed a skinny, pale woman coming down the stairs. She smiled falsely and walked over to him. Reaching out she led him by the hand up the stairs. She took him into a bedroom decorated in silvers and greys with a large four-poster bed. Closing the door behind her she walked up to Danny and ran her hands up his chest.

'What can I do for you, lover boy?' asked Ana in Romanian-broken-English.

Danny gently took her hands and sat her on the bed.

'Ana, I just want to talk to you.'

'Talk is okay. Some just want to talk first.'

'No, I need to ask you about the girl Yuri's men brought here,' Danny said calmly but poised to gag her if she shouted out.

'Who are you? I, I can't tell you, they will kill me,' she said, shaking, her eyes wide with fear.

'Shh, it's ok, listen to me. No one will ever know. Is she here? You know they are going to kill her.' Danny spoke softly keeping his eyes locked on hers.

She sat shaking, her eyes flicking from Danny to the door.

'Belek and Adrik came and took her this morning. Please, you can't tell anyone,' she said, tears welling up in her eyes.

'Ana, tell me all you know and I'll help you get out of here.'

'I can't. They have my passport. They will make my family suffer if I leave.'

'Look at me, you can trust me. If you help me, I'll help you. I promise,' said Danny, seeing a glimmer of hope come back into her eyes.

'What is she, your girlfriend, wife?'

'No, family, my cousin.'

'You promise you will help me?' asked Ana with a pleading look.

'You have to trust me. I'll get my cousin back and make sure the Volkovs never trouble you again.'

'Ok. I don't know where they took her. Adrik mentioned something about the factory to Belek.'

'The factory. Ok, anything else you can think of—places, people, anything?' Danny said, trying to gain anything useful.

'There is a safe in Viktor's flat. The TV swings out and it's behind it. Inside is a journal. It has all their business in it, times, places and money.'

'The safe, is it a key or combination lock?'

'It has a digital display with a keypad and a key. Viktor had one. I guess Yuri has it now. His cousin Dimitri has the other one. He always filled the journal in and looked after all the accounts,' said Ana, anxiously looking at the clock on the side.

'It's ok. Shit, a combination and a key.'

'I know the combination: 28-03-84. It was Viktor's date of birth. I have seen him enter it when he thought I was sleeping.'

'Good girl. Just tell me where Viktor's flat is and I'll get going.'

Ana told him the address and Danny went to leave. He turned at the door.

'Trust me, Ana, sit tight. I will be back for you, I promise.'

There was something about his voice and commitment that gave her hope. Seeing him leave she managed the first real smile since entering the country.

***

Out in the car Danny called Paul.

'Hi, Danny, what's up?' said Paul, answering straight away.

'I need some help, Paul,' replied Danny getting straight to the point.

'To do with Harry, and May's abduction, I suppose.'

Danny wasn't surprised Paul had heard about May's kidnap; his contacts went far and wide.

'Sorry, Paul. I can't really go into it now. I have some CCTV stills to send you. I need to know who's who, specifically which one is Yuri Volkov and which one is his cousin, Dimitri Volkov.'

'I can find out for you, but questions are going to be asked. How messy is this going to get?' asked Paul with concern in his voice.

'They cut her finger off, Paul.'

'I see. How long do you think?'

'He's still trying to make a point, make Harry suffer. I give it two days before she's dead,' said Danny, calm and business-like.

'I'll do what I can. Call me if you need anything. Any time, day or night.'

'Thanks, Paul. I'm sending the photos now.'

After they hung up, Danny went home. He needed food and a change of clothes before checking in on Trevor.

FORTY

Danny parked behind Tina's car and crunched up the gravel drive. As he turned the key he could see the glow of the kitchen light through the stained glass panels in the door. He was just about to shout his arrival when he sensed an unusual quietness about the house. A chill ran down his spine. Something was wrong. He'd only taken two steps towards the kitchen when a blow on the back of the head sent him into darkness.

***

His head felt heavy and his eyelids didn't want to open. Somewhere in his mind he registered two men talking. He couldn't understand what they were saying. Foreign? Russian. Forcing his eyes open he lifted his head through the searing pain from his crown.

'Ah, sleeping beauty is awake, da?' said Ivan, sitting on the kitchen worktop. Karl stood opposite him. Both of them held hunting knives in their hands; he noticed the guns partly visible in shoulder holsters under their open jackets. Danny moved his eyes around, past the large pots still bubbling away on the gas hob, past Tina's blender, past the kitchen table, until they fell on Tina and Rob. They were both gagged and tied to kitchen chairs, their eyes wide and scared, staring back at him, shaking in desperation as they struggled against their bonds. With his head clearing, Danny flexed his muscles subtly, barely noticeable. They'd taped his legs to the chair and his wrists to the chair's arms.

'Hey, big man, you remember me, da?' said Ivan, hopping down off the worktop. Danny's eyes locked firmly on him, his face taut and hard like stone.

Ivan thumped the knife down into the kitchen table and left it quivering as he moved in close to Danny.

'You stare at me all you want. You got lucky the first time we met. You not so lucky now, eh,' he said, stepping to one side to swing a heavy blow to the side of Danny's face. The blow knocked Danny sideways, rocking him on the chair before slumping him back down. He slowly raised his head to stare defiantly back at Ivan.

'Ha, good you stare. Keep watching,' Ivan said, pulling the knife out of the table and walking around towards Rob and Tina.

'I kill your brother, then I kill you. The woman we take. There are men who will pay good money for her,' he said laughing, and leered at Tina as she tried to shrink away from him.

Danny didn't reply. He'd felt the leg of the chair give a little after the punch. He was on the dodgy chair.

'Say goodbye to your brother,' said Ivan, bending over towards Rob, who was struggling to get free and freaking out at the sight of Ivan's knife.

Tensing with all his might, Danny deepened his breathing and with as much oxygen in the blood as he could get, he thrust his legs down in one explosive movement. The chair left the ground and landed at a tilt on its two back legs. His momentum and weight caused the wobbly chair to disintegrate into separate pieces, leaving him flat on his back.

Before Ivan could turn, Danny planted both his feet above him on the underside of the kitchen table. He thrust it with all his might, launching the heavy table at Ivan, knocking him over into the cooker. Danny was up into a kneeling position just in time to block Karl's knife with the arm of the chair still taped to his wrist. He brought his other arm around, striking Karl round the head with the chairs arm taped to the other wrist.

Out of the corner of his eye he saw Ivan going for his gun. Leaving Karl dazed he jumped up at Ivan, kneeing him in the face. The power of the blow crushed Ivan's barely-healed nose and fractured his jaw. He dropped like a stone, sending the gun clattering across the floor. Danny pulled the chair arms off his wrists and dropped to grab the gun. Before he got there an arm wrapped around his neck, dragging him back. A second later searing pain ran through his body as Karl thrust a knife into his side. He got a hand behind him onto Karl's wrist where they stayed in gridlock.

Danny couldn't get enough leverage to push Karl's hand away and Karl couldn't twist it in any further. Danny's other arm swung wildly around the kitchen worktop as Karl pulled tighter on his neck trying to choke him unconscious. He knocked the blender on, causing it to spin noisily, as he fought for air. Stars started to dance in front of his eyes.

Clamouring for focus Danny grabbed the shrieking blender and shattered the glass on the counter. As the last of the glass shards spun off the exposed blades, he rammed it backwards into Karl's face. Screaming through a spray of blood and bone and nose cartilage, Karl let go of the knife and Danny's throat in his panic. Gulping in a huge lungful of air Danny turned to finish Karl off. He only got a step when Ivan grabbed the back of his belt as he struggled to get up off the floor. Pulling Danny back, Ivan threw a powerful kidney-punch into Danny's side with his free fist. The blow hit him just below the knife still sticking out of his side. Danny folded over onto the kitchen worktop in crippling pain.

Focusing on the large pot on the cooker top, he grabbed it and threw the lava-hot stew all over Ivan's head. Yelling, he released Danny and frantically tried to clear his face from the blinding-hot agony. Just as Danny recovered enough to stand up, Karl charged him, screaming like a banshee. Fuelled with new-found adrenaline and fury, Danny side-stepped Karl's swinging fist and brought his knee up into his groin. As he doubled-up, Danny grabbed the back of his neck, thrusting his mutilated face down into the flaming gas hob. Karl screamed and jerked trying to pull away. His hair went up in a ball of flame as Danny held him down. When the hair had completely burnt off, and the movement slowly died away, Karl's knees gave way and he slumped to the floor.

Danny turned to see Ivan staring hatefully back through the one eye that could still see. His face was a mass of red-raw blisters. His scalded, blistered hands were struggling as he picked up his dropped gun and tried to pull the slide, he tried desperately to get a grip on the metal and chamber a round. Instinctively, Danny dropped as Ivan brought the gun round and fired. Hitting the floor, he pulled Karl's gun from under his jacket. As Ivan let more wild rounds off Danny rolled on his side and fired four shots in quick succession—two in Ivan's head and two in centre mass. The room went silent.

He lay there breathing heavily for a few minutes before dragging himself up. As he moved over to release Tina and Rob he stumbled slightly. His adrenaline levels were dropping, and pain was taking its place. The difficulty in moving reminded him he still had a knife stuck in his side. A hot, wet, burning from his shoulder led to the discovery of a deep, bleeding groove; one of Ivan's shots had clipped him as he'd dived to the floor.

FORTY ONE

He cut Tina and Rob free and stumbled back as they hugged each other in shocked relief. The whole scene of carnage had taken less than two minutes. Danny righted the kitchen table then slumped into a chair beside it. He moved his hand to get a shaky grip on the hilt of the knife in his side.

'Rob,' he said firmly to focus his brother. 'Rob, listen to me,' said Danny louder until he looked at him.

'Shit, Danny, sorry are you ok?' Rob let go of Tina and moved over to his brother, eyeing the knife uneasily.

'I need you to pull it out, Rob,' Danny said, moving his hand away.

'No, just sit tight. We need to call an ambulance and the police. We have—'

'ROB! You've gotta trust me. I need to get out of here or May's dead,' he said, gripping Rob's top and looking him squarely in the eyes.

'Tina, love, fetch me that tea towel and the roll of gaffer tape they tied us up with, it's over there in the corner.'

Tina pulled herself together and did as he asked. She opened the window on the way to let the acrid stench of burning flesh out.

'Pull the knife out, Rob, just a steady pull—not too quick,' said Danny, holding the tea towel round the wound.

Rob pulled it out as Danny put pressure on the wound through gritted teeth. Lifting his top and arm up, he got Rob to wind the gaffer tape around his middle, taping the tea towel tightly over the wound. After a few deep breaths, the pain dulled enough for him to take his top off and tape another tea towel over the bleeding groove in his shoulder.

'What the fuck's going on?' said Rob, staring at the dead bodies on the floor.

'There's no time to explain. You've just got to trust me,' said Danny pulling his wallet out. He took the picture of his wife and son out and then took his wedding ring and watch off, placing them on the table. Rob and Tina watched, puzzled.

'What do you want me to do?'

Danny knelt down with his hand on his side, grimacing as he pulled Karl's wallet out and pocketed it. Next he pulled a photo of his wife and child out of his own wallet and tucked it away before sliding his wallet into Karl's jeans, he grabbed Karl's arm and put his watch on it. Finally, he put his wedding ring on Karl's finger. Taking a few deep breaths he forced himself to search both bodies, pocketing the cash and gun magazines. Finding Ivan's mobile, he wiped the stew and dirt and blood off it. He grabbed Ivan's thumb and put it on the phone to unlock it. Seeing it ping into life he changed the thumb print to his own in case he needed it later. Seeing his brother's and Tina's shocked faces he picked up the guns and knives and put them on the table.

'I've got to disappear. It's the only way to save May. I need you to call the police and tell them this guy tied us up at gunpoint,' he said, pointing to Ivan.

'I got loose, and we fought. He dropped this gun in the scuffle. You got it, Rob. He killed me and came at you with the knife, you picked up this gun and shot him in self-defence,' said Danny, rolling Karl over to check his face was unrecognisable. Rob looked at him blankly, the shock making it hard for him to process Danny's instructions.

'Have you got that, bruv?' said Danny, cupping Rob's face, forcing him to focus.

'Yeah, yes I've got it. I'll call the police.'

'Tina, are you ok? Did you get that?' said Danny, looking past Rob.

Tina looked at him and nodded timidly. He put one of the guns in Rob's hand for fingerprints and one of the knives into Ivan's hand.

'Right, call the police,' Danny said, painfully pulling his top back on and tucking the cash, phone and magazines in his pockets. He tucked the gun and knife in the back of his jeans and went to leave.

'I'll call you, ok?'

'Danny,' Rob called, stopping him in the hall.

'Yeah.'

'Be careful.'

'Always am,' shouted Danny, shutting the front door behind him.

Rob hugged Tina tight and kissed her before picking up the phone.

FORTY TWO

It was late by the time DCI Nichola Swan parked her
Mini. She found an empty spot on the road, close to her
flat above Mr Kapour's crammed little mini market. She
went in and bought a bottle of wine before unlocking the
street door and climbing the stairs to the flats. Rattling
the key in her front door, she opened it and went inside.
Flicking on the light she threw her coat on the back of
the chair and kicked off her heels. She uncorked the
bottle and poured a large glass before padding through
to the lounge.

'Had a busy night?'

She froze, preparing to run, while her mind tried to
figure out who the shadowy figure in her armchair was.

'Fuck, you scared me. Shit. Yes, I've just spent the last
three hours investigating your death. Now what the fuck

are you doing in my living room?' she said warily, keeping the exit close behind her.

'Did DC Cripp turn up while you were there?' said Danny, ignoring her question.

'Err, yes, he was first on the scene. Why?'

'Who called him?'

She paused, thinking, while taking a large sip of wine.

'I don't know. I got the call from control. What are you getting at?'

'He was there because he gave my file to Yuri and was supposed to clean the scene or plant false evidence after he found us all dead,' said Danny leaning forward into the light, his blood-stained face looking tired and pale.

'Jonathan is on Yuri's payroll? He can't be!'

'I saw him on the CCTV from Silk & Lace. He was handing a file over to Yuri Volkov and taking a package in return.'

Danny looked down at the hand on his side. Nichola followed his eyes and saw the blood leaking out between his fingers.

'Jesus, what is it, gunshot wound?' she asked, disappearing into the kitchen.

'No, a knife. The one in the shoulder's a bullet wound.'

She reappeared a second later carrying a large first aid box.

'We should get you to a hospital.'

'You know I can't. At the moment they think I'm dead. It's the only chance I have to get May back alive and keep everyone around me safe.'

She knelt down in front of him and gently pulled the blood-soaked top over his head, before slowly peeling the gaffer tape off to look at the wound.

'You've lost a lot of blood. You need to get this stitched up,' she said, holding the blood-drenched tea towel back on it.

'Have you got a sewing kit?'

'No, I can't. I should arrest you not sew you—'

Before she finished the sentence, he swayed in the chair and fell forward on the floor unconscious.

***

He opened his eyes confused. The orange glow from a streetlight outside made its way through the curtains to light up the living room. His clothes were drying on an airer and Nichola Swan was curled up asleep in the armchair opposite. He lifted the duvet covering him, realising he was naked and all cleaned up. He tentatively sat up with the duvet round his waist and checked his side. It felt tender to touch but there wasn't any blood showing through the new white dressing. His shoulder stung a little as he moved but otherwise seemed ok; it was similarly dressed. Other than feeling a dull pain a little light-headed he seemed in pretty good shape.

'You're awake. How do you feel?' said Nichola moving over and kneeling in front of him. She slid her hands over his torso, checking the dressing over his knife wound. He couldn't help noticing how attractive she was. Her soft hands moved up to check the other dressing. Her long dark hair flowed over her shoulders in the same way her silky pyjamas flowed over her skin.

'A lot better, thanks.'

She looked up at him as she ran a hand over the scars on his torso.

'Shrapnel, knives and bullet wound scars. Your file says classified. What were you, Paras, a Seal or Special Forces?' she asked, her deep, dark eyes staring into his.

'Something like that,' he said with a wry smile before adding, 'Thanks for patching me up and washing my clothes.'

'Well, I had to do something to stop you bleeding all over my flat.'

They remained motionless, locked in a moment of indecision. She finally moved her head forward, her soft lips finding his. He responded as they kissed passionately, sliding his hand under her hair onto her back, pulling her towards him.

'Are you sure you're ok?' she asked, pulling away.

'I'm feeling better by the minute.'

She smiled back at him, unbuttoning her pyjama top and sliding the silky material off her shoulders.

FORTY THREE

A bang on the metal door of the old textile factory put
the two Serbian brothers on alert. They picked their
guns up off the table, relaxing at the sight of Dimitri on
the CCTV monitor. One of them slid the steel deadbolt
back and pulled the heavy sliding door open.

'Is Yuri here?' he asked walking past them without so
much as a look.

'He is downstairs with girls.'

Dimitri paced through the derelict factory. It had been
shut since the sixties, when a cheap influx of foreign
clothes had silenced the three floors of sewing machines.
Now, after several decades of neglect, the roof had
collapsed, causing the centre of the first and second
floors to rot and give way. This left a hole from the
concrete ground floor right up to the open sky. He
passed two more Serbians at the top of the stairwell, both

armed with AK submachine guns. They parted and let him descend to the basement. He thumped on another heavy metal door at the bottom. It creaked as it slid open to expose two further men, Russian this time.

Entering the basement was like entering a different building from the factory above. It was clinically clean with whitewashed walls and shiny, grey painted floor. The air-conditioner kept it at a comfortable twenty-two degrees, and its various rooms were all brightly lit by LED panels evenly spaced across the ceilings. Dimitri walked into a large room on the right and spotted Yuri in the centre. Women in white paper overalls worked on stainless steel catering tables that surrounded him. They formed production lines starting with brick packages of pure cocaine and heroin. As you followed the line, the girls cut and mixed the pure powder with a white mixture of chalk and fillers before weighing a few grams into little bags. None of them looked up or glanced at Dimitri or Yuri; their spirit had long since been beaten out of them, resigning themselves to their life of captivity.

'What did Cripp say?' demanded Yuri.

'Pearson got free and fought with Ivan and Karl. Ivan killed him. But Pearson's brother got Karl's gun and killed Ivan. They think he got Karl as well. There was a trail of blood leading out of the house.'

'Well, where the fuck is he?' said Yuri, raising his voice, his patience wearing thin.

'Nobody knows. Maybe he's holed up somewhere. Maybe he's dead. There was a lot of blood, he could have bled out,' said Dimitri warily.

'Fucking Harry Knight and his fucking family,' shouted Yuri, catching one woman looking his way.

With his temper getting the better of him, Yuri turned on her.

'You dare look at me, bitch,' he yelled, pulling his gun out with lightning speed. He squeezed the trigger without hesitation, sending a bullet straight through the centre of her forehead. An instant explosion of blood and brain glowed bright red across the white powder on the table behind her as the back of her head disintegrated. The room descended into shrieks as women cowered in fear.

'Who said you could stop working?' shouted Yuri, waving the gun around as he spoke. He walked out past Dimitri as the shaking women returned to work, tears rolling down their cheeks.

'Pasha. Pasha, where the fuck are you?'

'Yes, Boss,' called Pasha hurrying in from another room.

'Clear that shit up and get a replacement from Magda.'

Dimitri followed Yuri down the corridor to a locked door. He unlocked it and threw the door open. May's eyes looked up at him, wide and scared from a metal-framed bed at the back of the room. The chain padlocked tight around her waist to a metal ring on the wall rattled as she shook.

'Your cousin has cost me dearly,' said Yuri coldly, his emotions back in check.

'Good. When he finds you he's going to rip your balls off and make you eat them, you bastard,' she spat back at him, finding some of her father's spirit.

'That would be hard. Ivan ripped his face off and killed him.'

The news shattered her. She physically seemed to shrink into the bed. Yuri picked up the cutters from the table near the door and moved slowly towards her.

'Go look after the club, Dimitri, I will call you when I need you.'

Dimitri walked out of the room and back down the corridor. He glanced into the prep room to see Pasha wrapping the dead woman up in plastic. As he started up the stairs, May's blood-curdling scream echoed off the walls around him. Adrik came in as Dimitri was leaving. He nodded as they passed, his scarred face and cloudy blind eye shining in the shadowy factory. A demon from your worst nightmare.

FORTY FOUR

Danny woke in Nichola's bed to the sound of his mobile ringing. He glanced at the call ID before answering.

'Bob.'

'You all right, son? We heard what happened last night. I thought you were dead until I spoke to Rob. Those fucking Russian bastards.'

'I'm ok Bob. How's Harry bearing up?'

'He's going out of his mind not being able to do anything.'

'Actually, there is something I need you and Harry to do. I'll call you back in half an hour.'

Danny hung up, looking over at Nichola looking back at him. He leaned over and kissed her.

'There's a journal in a safe in Viktor's apartment. It has details of all the Volkov's activities, money, and all his businesses. You can have the journal after I've looked at it. Yuri is keeping May somewhere they call the factory.'

'I could try to get a warrant.'

'Nah, you've got no evidence or probable cause. You wouldn't get a search warrant granted. I've got a better idea,' he said getting out of bed and stiffly walking into the lounge to get his clean clothes. She followed after him, clicking on the kettle.

'Any plan that doesn't end in me being thrown off the force while taking down Volkov's organisation and busting DC Jonathan Cripp is good with me,' she said sarcastically while making the coffee.

'I'll need you to do a drugs raid at Silk & Lace later today, I'll let you know when. Whatever happens make sure Dimitri Volkov is taken into custody. When you bag his possessions, he will have the key to Viktor's safe on him. Get me the key and I'll do the rest. I'll have it back before his solicitor can get him out.'

'What if we don't find any drugs?'

'You will, and check the top drawer of the office desk, there's a loaded gun in it,' said Danny swigging down hot coffee. 'Sorry I've gotta go—time's short. I'll call you later,' he said, opening the door.

'Danny,' she called after him, panic in her voice.

'I know, last night, you and me. Mum's the word.'

'No, no. Be careful,' she said wrapping her arms around his neck and kissing him.

When she pulled back, Danny brushed her cheek with his hand.

'I'll call you later,' he said before disappearing down the stairs.

His phone was out and dialling before he reached the car.

'Bob, I need you and Harry to do something for m— What's all the commotion?' he said hearing Harry going ballistic in the background.

'The bastards sent another finger and a ransom note,' said Bob struggling to keep his anger in check.

'What does it say?'

'Ten million or they're going to kill her.'

'You know that's bollocks Bob. He's just playing with Harry; it's not about money, it's about making him suffer,' said Danny, picturing May alone and scared.

'Yeah, I know.'

'Put Harry on.'

The line went quiet for a minute until Harry came on.

'Danny, did you hear what that fucker's done to my little girl?'

'Harry, listen to me. I'm going to get May back, I swear. I'm up against time and I need you to do something for me.'

'If it helps get her back, anything,' said Harry regaining some of his usual form.

'Ok, listen carefully. This is what I need you to do.'

FORTY FIVE

Trevor jumped at the sound of the roller door opening. His muscles were cramping severely at being tied tightly in one position all night. His mouth was drier than he ever thought possible and he was freezing cold from lying on the concrete floor. He was expecting Danny to appear and cut him loose. Trevor figured if he was going to kill him, he would have done it by now. He felt the cable ties being snipped and stretched painfully. He felt hands slide up the back of the hood and remove the gag.

'About fucking time, you prick,' said Trevor though the hood.

They immediately threw him into a sitting position against the wall and pulled the hood off his head.

'Surprise, surprise, you stupid bastard.'

Trevor blinked, trying to focus after hours in the dark. As recognition kicked in he froze in terror. Harry Knight stood in the middle of four other men, a pump-action shotgun swinging loosely by his side. Trevor recognised the infamous Bob Angel to one side of him, a long-handled sledgehammer resting on one shoulder. The other men stood menacingly, armed with a machete, a hammer and a pickaxe handle.

'It wasn't me. I didn't kidnap May. It was Yuri's guys, Karl and Belek. I was just told to drive the van. I didn't know they were going to grab her,' said Trevor, his voice getting increasingly shaky.

'Shut up and listen. My nephew, Danny, is dead and your boss has got my daughter. He's cut off two of her fingers and I'm rather upset about it.'

Harry swung the shotgun up and pumped it to chamber a shell.

'You've got one chance of getting out of here without being cut up alive and fed to the lions at London Zoo.'

'Please don't. I'll do any—'

'I told you to shut up and listen. Bob, fucking snap his legs off,' said Harry as Bob took a step forward.

'No, no, I'm sorry. I'm listening. Please, I'll do anything,' cried Trevor, tears streaming down his face.

'Where's the factory?' barked Bob leaning in menacingly.

'What? Err I don't know where the factory is,' said Trevor, the verbal assault sending him further into a quivering mess.

'STOP FUCKING ABOUT. WHERE'S THE FACTORY?' bellowed Bob inches away from Trevor's face.

'I don't know. I'm sorry, only a few of Volkov's top-level men ever went there. It's in Central London somewhere, that's all I know. I'm sorry, please don't kill me.'

'Ok, stop snivelling and look at me. I want you to do something for me,' said Harry, his shotgun held firmly at his waist, levelled at Trevor.

'Anything, I'll do anything. You can trust me, I promise,' said Trevor, his self-preservation gene kicking in as he grasped the chance of getting out there alive.

'Right, good. Not that I don't trust an upstanding member of the community such as yourself. But I've taken out a little insurance. Show him, Bob.'

Bob put the sledgehammer down with a thud on the concrete floor, making Trevor jump out of his skin. He tapped his phone and turned it to show Trevor a picture. He could see his mum sitting terrified on the settee at home. Harry's men were sitting casually either side of her, one with a shotgun and the other with a silenced handgun.

'My associates here are going to take you to get cleaned up. Then Bob is going to tell you what you're going to do. You fucking listening to me, boy?' Harry yelled in Trevor's face.

'Yes, sorry yes, yes.'

'Right, do this and we're square. You go back to your shitty little life, ok? Fuck it up and they're going to find bits of you and your mum all over London. Got it?'

Trevor nodded slowly as Harry backed away. His boys grabbed him by the shoulders and dragged him off to a

Range Rover parked outside. Once they'd left Harry knocked on Scott's door. Danny answered it and beckoned them in. They followed him into the office where Scott had Silk & Lace's CCTV feeds up on screen.

'Thanks for your help, Scott. I won't forget this,' said Harry, peering over his shoulder.

'My pleasure, Mr Knight,' said Scott, smiling.

'Don't 'Mr Knight' me, Scott. I've known you since you were five years old running around with May and Danny in my garden. Call me Harry.'

'Ok, Harry, I'll do anything I can to get May back.'

'Right, that's enough of the pleasantries. Dimitri arrived about ten minutes ago. He's usually there for three or four hours checking the night's takings and doing the accounts. We need to get Trevor there for eleven o'clock. We'll give him a few minutes before I get the police in,' said Danny checking his watch as he walked through to the kitchen to call Nichola.

'We've gotta go. Thanks again, Scott. You ever need anything you let me know, ok?' he said patting Scott on the shoulder as they went out past Danny.

'Hold on a sec,' Danny said, putting the phone to his chest. 'As soon as I've got any news or if I need anything I'll call.'

Harry nodded and left. Danny got back to his call.

'You're all ready, yeah? Cripp doesn't know about the raid?'

'No, I pulled a favour and got him sent over to Wimbledon on a dead end house burglary,' said Nichola.

'Good. I'll see you round the back of the police station,' said Danny checking his watch again.

'Mm, I look forward to it,' she said seductively.

'Yeah all right. If I manage to live through this, there'll be plenty of time for that later,' he said with a chuckle.

'Spoilsport. I'll see you later.'

Danny went back through to Scott and looked at Dimitri sitting upstairs in his office.

'Gotta go, Scotty boy. Keep an eye on Dimitri for me. Call me if he goes to leave or anybody suspicious comes in before the police turn up.'

'Absolutely, old boy. I'll catch up with you later,' said Scott excited to be involved.

Wheelspinning off the gravel drive, Danny left in his borrowed Mercedes.

FORTY SIX

Dimitri's head was pounding as he sat at his desk. He popped a couple of aspirin in his mouth and swilled them down with a glass of water. He'd been checking last night's takings but was finding it hard to concentrate. This business with Yuri and Harry Knight had given him a massive headache. He was a Volkov and understood that family honour meant Yuri had to avenge Viktor's death. But torturing Knight's daughter and killing his nephew was drawing way too much attention to their business. Runners had gone missing and customers were nervous about the additional police activity. He wished Yuri would just kill the man and be done with it. Instead, Yuri planned to make Knight suffer a little longer before luring him to a ransom exchange. Then Yuri wanted to kill his daughter in front of Knight before killing him and taking his head home to satisfy his father. The business with Pearson bothered him. The police weren't fools; they would soon link Ivan to them, and when they found Karl—either dead or alive—his record in Russia would link him to Yuri. A knock on the office door distracted him enough to shake the bad feeling away.

'Come in,' he shouted, rubbing his forehead.

Trevor peered around the door and walked in sheepishly.

'Where the hell have you been? You missed last night's drops.'

'Yeah, sorry, the police were all over the estate doing stop searches. I had to stash the gear. I've only just had a chance to pick it up,' said Trevor as convincingly as possible.

He reached into his rucksack and pulled out a package and placed it on the desk. Dimitri recoiled like it carried the plague.

'Why the fuck have you brought it here? You never bring anything to the club. NEVER.'

'Sorry, it's been a long night, and I couldn't get hold of Ivan,' said Trevor apologetically.

Dimitri picked up the package and started around the desk.

'Here, take it and fuck off. I'll get someone to pick it up later.'

He'd got within a few feet of Trevor, when the door burst open and the drug squad poured in.

'Stay where you are. Keep your arms where I can see them.'

Dimitri did as he was told without saying a word. His eyes just burned furiously at Trevor, who shrank back in the knowledge he was a marked man. As soon as they were handcuffed DCI Nichola Swan entered the room.

'Dimitri Volkov and Trevor Bailey, I'm arresting you for the possession of class A drugs with intent to deal.'

She looked past Dimitri at the officer behind the desk. He nodded back as he pulled the handgun out of the drawer.

'I'm also arresting you for the possession of an illegal firearm. That's a five stretch right there, Mr Volkov.'

She produced a clear plastic evidence bag and held it while an officer rifled through Dimitri's pockets placing the contents in the bag. She did the same with Trevor while other officers bagged up the drugs and the gun.

Dimitri continued to say nothing as they led him out of the room in handcuffs. He stared at Trevor, shaking his head slowly from side to side. DCI Swan followed behind, slipping Dimitri's key chain out of the evidence bag and into her jacket pocket.

***

An hour later Nichola climbed into the passenger seat next to Danny. She smiled at him and pulled out a bunch of keys.

'This is all he had on him so I hope it's here.'

'Only one way to find out,' said Danny taking them off her.

'What if someone's there?' she said, putting her arm on his.

'I'll figure it out as I go. I can't let the Russians know I'm still alive. If Yuri finds out, he's liable to kill May on the spot then go for Harry. How long have I got with the keys?'

'Dimitri's already called his sleazebag solicitor, David Wilkins. He's got to get here first, then he'll argue the drugs were Trevor's or they found them in the club, or some other bullshit to get him off. We can't prove the gun is his and he'll probably say it was Viktor's; as he's dead that's the end of that. I reckon I can keep them for three hours maximum. Get the keys back here in two to be safe.'

Danny leaned in and kissed her. 'I better get going then,' he said with a cheeky grin.

FORTY SEVEN

Danny looked up from behind a neighbouring wall. Viktor's apartment was twelve storeys above him, at the top of a new apartment building. It was impossible to tell if anyone was in from outside. He moved to the entrance foyer and turned his attention to the ring of keys.

Two or three of them could be safe keys. Plenty of Yale keys that could be for the apartment door.

He checked his watch.

Twenty minutes gone already, better get on with it.

The entrance door had a TV screen and a keypad for visitors to dial apartments. Below the keypad was a plastic pad with a picture of a key on it. He picked a grey plastic fob on the key chain and tapped it on the pad. The door lock buzzed, allowing him to enter. With the clock ticking, he ignored his natural instinct to take the stairs and found a similar keypad in the lift. He tapped the fob, lighting up the buttons, allowing him to select the penthouse floor. Poking his head out at the top, there were only two penthouses and no one around. He walked over to Viktor's apartment door and gently placed his ear on it. No sound, no TV, no voices. He stood motionless for several minutes. Breathing shallow, tuning out the corridor noise, he concentrated on the sounds inside the apartment. Nothing.

Shuffling through the keys he found one that turned, clicking the lock open. Sliding inside he locked the door behind him. Wasting no time, he worked quietly through the rooms, checking each one in case someone was sleeping, dressing, or showering. Satisfied, he picked up the pace and made for the TV. Swinging it away from the wall he found the safe staring back at him, plain and grey and larger than he was expecting. He rattled through the keys, relieved to find one that fit the lock. Twisting it produced a satisfying clunk.

When he typed the code into the keypad it beeped, allowing him to pull the two-foot-square door open. The safe was deep, containing several files and the journal. Stacked behind the paperwork, filling it from top to bottom was a wall of money bundles. Danny took one out and flicked it through his fingers. All used fifties banded in twenty-five thousand pound bundles. He tossed it to one side and grabbed the journal. He'd planned to take pictures on his phone before putting it back to cover his tracks, but there was way more information in the journal than he'd expected. The files contained documents and information on deals, property, and transactions. Glancing around, Danny moved through the apartment, opening cupboards and wardrobes until he found a large sports holdall. He put the files and journal in the bottom then paused looking at the money.

Fuck it, they owe me a new kitchen.

He packed the money in until he could only just close the zip. The last three bundles had to go in his jacket pockets. With the safe and TV back into position, Danny checked his watch and made his way to leave. His hand touched the apartment door handle and froze. He could hear voices approaching from the lift.

Shit.

Backing away he left the lounge as the key rattled in the lock, easing into the master bedroom as the apartment door closed. He left the bedroom door ajar, just enough to see who entered the lounge in the reflection off the hall mirror. His body tensed when Yuri and Adrik moved into view. He placed the sports bag on the floor, keeping his eyes locked on Yuri and Adrik as he eased the door open. Tensing his legs he readied himself to go, the order of attack already playing out in his head.

Three, two, one, wait.

Three more men moved into view, frustrating Danny. He exhaled, closing the door back to a crack. Two armed men with the element of surprise had a high chance of success, five armed men was suicide, however much he wanted to get at Yuri Volkov. He looked at his watch.

Time's running out. I need to get the keys back to Nichola.

Peering through the gap, the reflected face of DC Jonathan Cripp came into view. With his ear close to the door, he listened as voices grew louder.

'What the fuck do we pay you for, huh?' said Adrik, uncomfortably close to Jonathan's face.

'DCI Swan organised the raid. Someone kept me out of the loop. I wasn't told about it,' said Cripp stuttering nervously.

'That's not good enough and where's Karl? You still haven't found him,' said Adrik, keeping up the pressure as the other two men moved in behind Cripp.

'Well, if you didn't go around kidnapping people and destroying half of London, I wouldn't have the super on my ass, would I?'

Cripp immediately regretted his outburst. Yuri had a gun against his forehead before he could blink.

'Don't make me question your usefulness, Cripp.'

The room went silent as Cripp went whiter than a sheet.

'No, of course not, Yuri. I'm sorry. I just keep coming up against DCI Swan. She's like a dog with a bone when it comes to you and Knight.'

Yuri dropped the gun and moved away. Turning his back to Cripp he looked out the window across the Thames to the city skyscrapers.

'Then you will to have to get rid of her,' he said.

Danny looked at his watch as he heard Cripp protesting weakly in the background. Time was up. He had to go. He moved quietly back and opened one of the glass doors, just enough to slide through onto the bedroom terrace.

***

In the living room Yuri cocked his head towards the bedroom. A faint breeze caught his cheek and the noise of the city, although hard to distinguish, had got very slightly louder.

***

On the terrace Danny searched for a way down. He was hoping for a fire escape or a way across to the other penthouse apartment, but nothing presented itself. Moving along the terrace with his back against the lounge wall, he got to the end and swung his head around to peep in through the window. He could see the men still intimidating Cripp. Behind them he saw Yuri, his head fixed on the bedroom door.

Shit!

***

Yuri levelled his gun on the bedroom, the conversation behind him coming to an abrupt halt. Adrik instinctively raised his gun and followed his boss. Side-stepping to the door, Yuri stared down the gun barrel through the gap. He jerked his head towards the door, beckoning Adrik to enter the room. Bursting in Adrik swept to one side while Yuri covered the other.

Adrik appeared a second later from the en-suite bathroom and shook his head. Yuri lowered his gun, pausing momentarily before raising it again and moving towards the terrace door.

***

Danny had seen them enter the bedroom as his head lowered out of sight. Hanging by his fingertips off a girder below the balcony, Danny peered down fixing his eyes on the balcony rail of the apartment below. His heart pounded as he heard the door above open. An approaching ambulance drowned out the sound of Yuri's footsteps above. Seizing the moment Danny dropped, throwing his arm forward to hook over the railing of the apartment below. As he fell through the air the weight of the bag on his back pulled him off balance. He hit the rail with his elbow instead of hooking it, the blow knocked him back into open air as he fell towards the ground. A mixture of blind panic and survival instinct kicked in. He shot his arm out, grabbing the rail of the next balcony down. Gripping with everything he had he held fast, his shoulder almost coming out its socket. As the realisation he wasn't dead sank in, he swung his other arm up and hauled himself over. Landing in a heap on his back he laid there breathing heavily.

***

Two floors above, Yuri moved to the rail. He looked over at the wailing ambulance and watched it disappear noisily around the corner. He glanced down at the twelve-floor drop, then turned slowly and returned to the apartment.

FORTY EIGHT

With his heart rate and breathing returning to normal, Danny pulled himself up, the knife wound and his shoulder complaining bitterly as he did so. Checking the apartment was empty he pulled the gun out and struck the glass door hard with the butt, shattering it into thousands of tiny fragments. He walked through peeling some fifties off the bundle in his pocket, throwing them on the sofa as he went past. Checking the corridor was clear he crossed and left the building down the stairwell. Back in the car he checked his phone to see two missed calls from Nichola. He put it on hands-free and hit the redial button while hurtling his way towards the police station.

'It's me, I'm on my way back now,' he said when she answered.

'Did you get the pictures of the journal?' she said in a hushed voice.

'No, there was too much to photograph. I had to take the lot.'

'Ok, good, but get back here pronto. I can't stall them for much longer. Wilkins is ripping us apart and demanding immediate release,' Nichola said hanging up.

Fifteen minutes of erratic driving later, Danny parked around the corner from the police station and text Nichola. She appeared hurrying around the corner a minute later. He handed her the keys through the window.

'About time, slowcoach,' she said, taking them off him and turning to hurry back in.

'Nichola!' Danny shouted, stopping her in her tracks.

'What? Hurry up.'

'When you finish today, don't go home.'

She looked at him strangely, his expression and tone making her take him seriously.

'Why?'

'Yuri's ordered Cripp to get rid of you,' he said, pulling Karl's gun out and offering it to her. 'Take this and lie low for a bit. It'll soon be over.'

'No, I'm in this until the end, but thanks for the warning,' she said, shaking her head as she walked back to the car. She leaned in through the window and kissed him hard on the lips.

'Ok, but be careful. I'll call you as soon as I can.'

'I still want that journal,' she said with a smile.

'Don't worry you'll get it.'

She turned away rushing back to the station. He watched her go then drove away, dialling the phone as he went.

'Paul, it's Danny. I need your help, mate.'

'Danny, I wondered when the dead would rise,' said Paul in a sarcastic tone.

'A necessary diversion, mate. May's life depends on it.'

'What do you need?' said Paul, turning serious.

'I'll be there in twenty minutes.'

Danny hung up and put his foot down.

FORTY NINE

Reaching the top of the stairs Danny looked around for
Trisha at reception. She was nowhere in sight so he
moved towards Paul's office.

'I sent her home. Be a good chap, pop downstairs and
flick the lock on the door. I'd rather we weren't
disturbed,' shouted Paul before Danny got to his door.

'Ok,' Danny answered, already halfway down the
stairs.

On his return, he found Paul sitting behind his desk
waiting for him, a mug of hot coffee for each of them on
the top.

'Ouch, you look like you've been hit by a bus,' said
Paul stretching across to shake Danny's hand.

'Yeah, well I wish I had, it would have hurt less,' said
Danny with a grin.

He threw the sports bag on the chair and unzipped it. Digging his hands in he tumbled cash bundles out onto the desk until he could get to the files and journal. He pushed the cash to one side and put the paperwork down on the desk with a thump.

'Well, what have we got here, then?' asked Paul with a raised eyebrow.

'I'll come to that in a minute. First, who's the best guy you've got?'

'Apart from you, Matthew West. Navy Seal, tough as they come.'

'Next best.'

'Curtis Fenn, ex-parachute regiment. What do you need them for?' asked Paul, not sure if he wanted to hear the answer.

'I just need them to watch over somebody, discreetly. If she's in trouble I need them to step in. They'll need to be armed, we're dealing with serious criminals,' said Danny sitting down and waiting while Paul sat back thinking for a second.

'Ok, but that kind of heat will cost you.'

'Fine, take it out of this lot. But I need them on it like yesterday,' said Danny, waving bundles of cash at Paul.

'I'll call them now. Who are they babysitting?'

'DCI Nichola Swan. Here, I'll write her address down.'

Paul raised his eyebrow once again then picked up the phone. Fifteen minutes and two calls later Paul put it down again.

'It's done; they're on the way to the station now. They'll follow her wherever she goes from there, ok?'

'Good, thanks Paul,' said Danny, relaxing a little as he picked up the journal.

'Somewhere in this lot is an address for something Yuri Volkov calls the factory. He's holding May there.'

Paul picked up a file and opened it, looking at Danny. 'I guess we better get to work then,' he said, smiling.

They worked as the sky drew dark outside. Danny checked through the files, spreading them out on the tables. They had full records of shipping container deliveries and port authority documents for sealed goods consignments. Coffee from Columbia, powdered milk from Russia, nuts and other goods... the list went on. Danny assumed it was Volkov's gateway for the drugs into the UK. Paul worked methodically through the journal, making notes as he went. They referred to all Volkov's illegal dealings, using simple name changes for products: coffee and loose tea for cocaine and heroin, livestock for trafficked women, with the country of origin besides them.

Danny got up to make more coffee and swayed, leaning on the desk for support. The wound in his side was ripping pain through his body. He took a few deep breaths until it passed then stood again. His head swam, the dizziness sending him down on one knee. Paul's arm was around him before he fell, helping him onto the sofa in the office corner. He lifted Danny's top to see a mass of bruising and the bandaged knife wound, a red blemish covering the middle of the white bandage.

'First, we've got to clean this up, then you need to rest,' said Paul, grabbing the first aid kit from the kitchen.

'I can't. I've got to get May back.'

'If you don't rest now, you won't be getting anyone back,' said Paul, pushing him back on the sofa.

Danny gave in to exhaustion as Paul cut off the old dressing and cleaned the knife wound.

'Hmm, your needlework's better than I remember,' said Paul, studying the black cotton stitches.

'Not mine, mate,' said Danny with a cheeky grin.

'Ah, let me guess, DCI Nichola Swan.'

Danny didn't answer but his continued grin said it all.

'You need to get that looked at, old chum. It looks infected,' said Paul, wiping the weeping wound before bandaging it back up again.

'I will, as soon as this is over.'

'Ok, ok, rest for a bit. I'll keep working through the journal.'

Danny lay his head back intending on getting up after a quick catnap. His eyes closed and he fell into a deep sleep in seconds. An hour later Paul had pictured and scanned a series of documents and pages from the journal into his computer. He tagged them into an email and picked up the phone.

'Howard, it's Paul. The subject of yesterday's conversation has turned up.'

'Really? That's another tenner I owe you. How is he?' he said in his perfect English accent.

'A bit banged up. He's sleeping at the moment,' said Paul, finishing the email as he spoke.

'Has he found her yet?'

'No, which brings me to why I'm calling. I'm sending you an email now. It contains a dozen or so delivery notes and pictures of a journal belonging to the Volkovs. I need you to check them out and find me one that would match a place called the factory.'

'Is that where he's—' said Howard, his voice going up a pitch.

'Danny seems to think that's where he's holding her.'

There was silence on the line.

'You still think we should let him keep going?'

'It solves your problem with the Russians, and I don't know of anyone better to get May back,' said Paul, calm and emotionless.

'Hmm, ok, go with it. Anything else you need? said Howard giving his blessing.

'Yes, I'm sending you a list now. I need it urgently before he wakes up. Because once he's awake there won't be any stopping him.'

'Consider it done. Is that it?' asked Howard, reading Paul's emails as he spoke.

'One last thing. Your suspicions of DC Cripp were right. I have a list of payoffs and evidence tampering here. I also have two men watching DCI Swan. Cripp has been ordered to get rid of her by Volkov. I'd like your blessing to use whatever force is needed to keep her safe.'

Howard went silent again as he took it in.

'Ok fine, as long as there's no loss to civilian life. I'll have DC Cripp picked up and detained.'

'Thank you, Howard,' said Paul, putting the information regarding Cripp to one side.

'No, thank you, Paul. I'll see you at the club tomorrow. Bring all the information with you. We'll take it from there.'

The phone went dead leaving Paul in the semi-dark office watching his friend sleep on the sofa.

FIFTY

A battered old Ford Transit van sat parked on the opposite side of the road, a little way back from the mini market. It had its back doors to the streetlight, leaving the cab cloaked in shadows. Curtis Fenn and Matthew West sat motionless in the darkness, trained and focused as they watched Nichola's flat and the approaching road. West's phone buzzed in his pocket. He tapped his earpiece without getting it out. He didn't want the glow to light the cab up.

'Yep.'

'It's Paul. All quiet?'

'Yeah, an old BMW with four blokes in it pulled up about forty minutes ago. It sat there for five minutes then drove off.'

'What did they look like?'

'Bruisers, street thugs; definitely not professionals.'

'Ok, keep on it. The man from Whitehall has given you his blessing. Whatever's needed as long as civilians don't get hurt.'

'Ok, Boss. I'm guessing they'll be back after the mini market shuts. Who's the client?' asked West curiously.

'He's one of the good guys, Matt. He saved me from getting my head chopped off in Afghanistan.'

'Good enough for me, Boss,' said West, ending the call.

They sat there silent and still in the dark, eventually watching Mr Kapour turn the lights off and lock the shop. The minutes ticked slowly by in the quiet street. The BMW returned just before 1:00am.

'About time. I was about to die of boredom,' said Fenn, his eyes never leaving the BMW.

Three men got out, crossed the road, and stood outside the door leading up to the flats. They left the driver in the car with the engine still running.

'As soon as they go in, I'll give you ten to pop the driver and meet me at the door,' said West, checking the silencer on his gun.

'Gotcha. Any second now,' said Fenn, clicking the door open a crack, ready. Nobody saw him as he slid out, the interior light being disabled when they stole the van earlier. He approached the back of the BMW fast and low, masked by the parked cars lining the street.

***

Nichola's eyes shot open, she was fully awake before her head left the pillow. She'd only been asleep a short while, Danny's warning of Yuri's death threat playing heavy on her mind. There had been a sound. She hadn't consciously heard it, but she knew it had woken her. Sitting up on the side of the bed she listened, trying to filter out the normal sounds of the flat and quieten the pounding of her heart. There it was, the faint thump and rattle of the chain on the door downstairs being forced. Picking up her police-issue taser and baton, Nichola tiptoed into the lounge and stopped. Another sound, the creak of the loose step near the top of the stairs. She tried to steady her shaking hands as she moved through the kitchen towards the entrance door. She heard the creak of the step again and again two seconds later.

Three people. Shit—there's three of them.

Her mind raced. The flimsy Yale lock on her front door wouldn't stop them for long. With gritted teeth she ran through options. If she rushed them at the top of the stairs, perhaps she could taser one and push him on top of the others as they came up the stairs. She moved to the hall and heard people moving outside; they were trying to be quiet but weren't quite achieving it. Nichola breathed heavily as she psyched herself up for the charge. With her hand shaking as it rested on the lock, she heard new sounds... faintly echoing through the door: metallic pings and the dull thuds. Was it... people falling? More movement now... Low grunts and footsteps on the stairs. She backed away confused and terrified. She crouched in the corner opposite with her taser gun raised in her trembling hands. Then nothing. No sound, no killers charging through the door. Nothing but silence. The sounds of the flat returned to their peaceful tick.

Seconds passed. Minutes passed. After a full fifteen minutes Nichola moved tentatively to the door. She opened it slowly to see an empty landing. Creeping forward she peeped over the banister and looked down at the stairs. An eerie orange glow of the street lamp outside made its way through the open front door. She moved slowly down the stairs, still not wanting to expose herself by turning on the light. She stepped round blood on the stair carpet; it looked like black tar in the orange glow. Standing at the bottom Nichola peered out of the open door. The street was deserted. An old BMW sat across the road, its driver's door open, a steamy smoke trail floating out of the exhaust as the engine ticked over.

As if shocked into action, she slammed the front door and ran up the stairs to the flat. Running to the bedroom she started to dress and pack a bag as quickly as she could, itching to get the hell out of there fast. The second the front door had shut, the battered old Ford Transit started up and drove slowly past, its headlights only coming on once Fenn had turned left, driving out of sight of Nichola's flat.

FIFTY ONE

The images of Ivan and Karl attacking him in his mum's kitchen shocked Danny upright in a cold sweat. He breathed heavily, pushing the ghosts away.

'Morning,' said Paul, moving to the small office kitchen.

'Shit, what time is it?'

'Slow down there a minute, you need something to eat or you're not going to be any good to anyone,' said Paul clinking away out of sight.

'The factory. Did you find the address of the factory?' asked Danny, rising unsteadily from the sofa. It suddenly dawned on him he'd hardly eaten anything for two days.

'Yes, I've got it, sit down,' said Paul, coming back into the office with a big mug of coffee and a plate piled with freshly microwaved pizza.

'All I've got I'm afraid. I ordered in last night but thought it best to let you sleep.'

Paul handed them over to Danny who demolished the plateful at a record pace. Feeling refreshed he moved over to Paul's desk, glugging down hot coffee as he went.

'What you got, Paul?'

'An old clothes factory. It's been empty since the late sixties. A shell company out of Croatia, owned by the Volkov family, bought it two years ago.'

'What's all these?' said Danny picking up plans off the desk.

'The original architect plans courtesy of City of Westminster planning office.'

'What? How the hell did you get all this in the middle of the night?' said Danny running through the individual floor plans.

'Let's just say I have certain acquaintances who have a mutual interest in seeing the Volkovs driven out of London. Unfortunately for political reasons they can't be seen to be involved in their removal, which brings me to something I have over here that may interest you,' said Paul, pointing to a large khaki kit bag propped up in the corner. Danny got up slowly, the pain in his side worse than last night. Beads of sweat speckled on his forehead.

'You should be in hospital,' said Paul noticing his pain.

'If I live through this, it's my first port of call,' said Danny in a poor attempt at humour.

He opened the bag and a big grin spread across his face despite his discomfort.

'I think the odds of that hospital appointment just got a little higher,' he said as he pulled out a suppressed automatic weapon and a bulletproof vest. Delving deeper he pulled out more equipment. He laid them all out, flash-bangs, ammunition, handguns and knives.

'Thanks, Paul. I owe you one.'

'No, I rather think we'll just call it quits. Now go and get May.'

***

One of the Harry's guys gave Bob the jiffy bag at the door. Dreading its contents he took it through to the lounge. Harry sat in an armchair, dishevelled and red eyed, still in yesterday's clothes. Gripping a whiskey glass in one hand and the empty bottle in the other, he looked at Bob and the jiffy bag.

'Just open it, Bob.'

Ripping off the top, Bob did as Harry asked. He looked in to see one of May's little fingers and a note. He took the note out and read it to Harry.

'Bring the money to hangar number seven, North Weald Airfield at 2:00pm. Just you and Angel. Come alone or I'll cut your daughter's head off and mail it to you,' Bob spoke calmly, keeping a lid on days of anger and frustration as best he could.

Harry looked at him a broken man. His eyes focused on the jiffy bag as he spoke.

'Did he hurt her again?' he said, his eyes welling up. Bob nodded grimly.

'Is the last of the money together?'

'Yeah, Jimmy lent us the last £700k with the Dog up as security.'

'You heard from Danny?' asked Harry with a glimmer of hope.

'Not yet, but there's still time,' said Bob, looking at his phone as if the mention would make it ring.

'If we don't hear from him in the next couple of hours we'll have to go.'

'Shall I round up the boy's boss?'

'No, that bastard will be watching for that. If we turn up mob-handed he'll kill May before we get within a mile of him,' said Harry, his anger sparking some fight from within once more. 'But that won't stop us going tooled up. Get us some serious fucking firepower, Bob. First chance I get, I'm gonna blow that Russian fucker off the face of the earth. I'm off for a shower. Phone Danny before we leave just in case he's found May.'

'Ok, Boss,' said Bob already going through his phone to arrange the guns.

'Bob, you know you don't have to come with me,' said Harry with a look that said he meant it.

'What and leave you on your own? You wouldn't even find the airfield,' said Bob, managing a smirk.

Harry smiled back. There was nobody he'd rather have with him than Bob. It felt better to be tackling this head-on than carry on with the endless pain of the last few days.

FIFTY TWO

Danny parked in a side road opposite the old factory. He took the crumpled picture of his wife and child out of his pocket and held it on the steering wheel. He stared at it a while before looking up and focusing on the task ahead.

The building looked derelict and abandoned. He would have said Paul had got it wrong if it wasn't for the shiny CCTV cameras covering the large, rusty sliding door. At first appearance it looked corroded and disused but with a closer look they'd greased the wheels and the rail was shiny from frequent use.

No going in through there. I need to get in some other way. Undetected, quietly.

If they heard him coming they would either kill May or use her against him. Looking up he could see through one of the upstairs windows. Sunlight streamed in through a large collapsed section of roof.

That's my way in.

His eyes flicked back to the photo. He felt a pang of guilt at the thought of Nichola and the crazy last few days. It was the first time since their deaths that he'd not thought about them every second of the day. He put the photo back in his pocket, his face hardening and eyes focusing, the emotional switch turning off in his head as he readied himself for battle.

An office block lay behind the factory, converted from a similar building and attached to its rear wall. Its entrance was at the opposite end to the factory, around the corner on Canning Road. Danny made his way to its reception, beads of sweat on his forehead as he walked, from wearing a large canvas jacket to cover the multitude of arms and kit. He knew he may not win this, but he wasn't going to go down without a fight.

Standing outside the office building he waited until a group of people entered. While they were busy talking to the young girl on reception, he entered and scooted past, moving off to the stairs. Most people used the lift, so the stairwell was empty. Running up three at a time to the top floor, he glanced around and moved up the final flight to a locked door leading to the roof. He tried shouldering it, but it held fast. He looked down the empty stairwell as he unzipped his jacket. Drawing his silenced Glock he popped off three rounds, obliterating the wood around the lock. The door swung open with a tap.

Moving to the roof edge he looked down. It was only a two-metre drop to the factory roof. In its centre he could see the collapsed middle section with a hole in it. Turning, Danny went back down to the fourth floor. He waited in the stairwell, watching through the fire doors, until all the office workers moved out of the corridor and into the lift. When it was clear he opened the red emergency door to the fire hose. Unhooking it off the reel, he cut it free with his commando knife and moved back up to the roof. Losing the jacket, he threw the hose onto the factory roof, strapped the silenced Uzi machine gun across his back and dropped down. He landed heavily with the weight of the kit, aggravating the pain in his side. As he stood he had to steady himself as his head swam. It passed in a moment but told him the infection in his side was getting worse. Sucking it up, he moved towards the hole in the centre, crawling the last few feet to peer into the deserted second floor.

The roof creaked a little near the opening but seemed solid enough to take his weight. Tying the end of the hose around an exposed girder, he slid down to the second floor. Debris from the roof collapse had ripped a hole all the way through to the ground floor. Wrapping the hose around his leg he lowered himself upside down through the hole, just enough to check that the first floor was empty. He was starting to think he really did have the wrong place as he slid down to the first floor. Landing with his feet on the edge of the hole, it dislodged some loose debris which fell through to the ground floor, clanging loudly as it landed. Danny swung himself and the hose away from the hole, just as shouts and voices came from below. Treading carefully he moved back looking for another way down.

'Nah, is nothing. Just more crap falling from the roof,' came a voice from the ground floor.

'Ok, leave it. Yuri will be here soon to take the girl.'

Danny stopped and turned his head at the mention of May. Remembering the plans of the building, he moved to a stairwell in the far corner. It led all the way down to a small basement room, which had to be where they were holding May. Looking over the stair rail, he could see the basement below. He couldn't see anyone on the stairs so he made his way down, one flight at a time. He crouched to peep under the door arch into the ground floor. Three armed guards stood with their backs to him. They talked and smoked, relaxed and unaware he was there. With his knife in one hand and his finger on the trigger of the Uzi in the other, he crept down the stairs, one gentle footstep at a time. He noted two more armed men by the sliding door on the far side as he passed them, silently descending to the basement.

FIFTY THREE

At the bottom of the stairs the basement opened out to
the ten-by-ten metre room Danny had seen on the plans.
His heart sank at the sight of the empty room. The
feeling was quickly pushed aside by the sight of a sliding
metal door that wasn't on the plans. He walked over to
it, surprised to see it slide back before his eyes. Staring
back at him in equal surprise was Pasha. He moved to
raise his gun and open his mouth at the same time.
Danny reacted quickly, clamping Pasha's mouth and
stabbing him up between the ribs and into his heart.
Grabbing feebly onto Danny's arms, Pasha stared at him
with panicking eyes, his legs already starting to buckle.
Danny gripped him as he went down, his hand still
clamped tightly over his mouth. Pasha convulsed and
twitched before dying seconds after hitting the floor.
Danny looked up, grateful no one was alerted, and

surprised at the large, brightly lit basement spread out in front of him. Rooms led off the large corridor in each direction. Grabbing Pasha under the arms he dragged him to the void under the stairs and tucked him in out of sight. Moving into the basement that wasn't on the plans, he slid the metal door shut behind him. His hand shook slightly as he let go of the handle, and he felt cold even though he was sweating heavily.

Pull yourself together, Danny.

He moved forward, close to the wall, and darted a look through the glass in the first door. Women were busy working production lines, cutting and bagging drugs while two armed men watched over them. Danny moved on to the next room. This was empty and set out like a prison dormitory for the women workers. He didn't dwell on that, just moved on past store rooms and a kitchen to the last door. Drawing back the big deadbolt he pulled it open. In the gloom he could see someone on a bed in the corner. He'd taken a couple of paces into the room, when he sensed someone come at him from the side. His gun was up with the trigger finger already squeezing as his eyes locked with Ana's.

'It's you. I waited, you didn't come,' she said, lowering the chair from above her head down.

'Well, I'm here now,' replied Danny, moving to the figure on the bed.

'May, it's Danny,' he said, moving her hair away so she could see him. Her pupils were large and dilated. She mumbled to herself before a flicker of recognition lit up her face.

'Danny, they said you were dead. Am I dead?' she slurred.

'They keep her drugged to keep her quiet—the pain in her hands, you know,' said Ana, pointing to her bandaged fingers. 'They bring me here to look after her.'

'Give me a hand with her, Ana and I'll get you both out of here.'

'Danny, are we going home?' said May fighting to find focus.

'Yes, May, we're going home.'

He moved to the door and checked the corridor. It was still clear. With her arm around May, Ana followed behind. Danny pulled one of his handguns from its holster, chambered a round and took the safety off. He handed it to Ana, who took it without hesitation.

'Anyone comes at us, just shoot for the chest. Don't think, just shoot, ok?'

Ana had a determined look on her face as she nodded and followed him. They ducked under the windowed door to the production line and reached the metal exit door. He slid it open a couple of feet, only to see Yuri and Adrik with two guards coming down the last few steps. Danny just managed to push everyone behind the door, sliding it shut as a hail of bullets whizzed through the closing gap and thudded into the back of the door. Dents like half ping-pong balls peppered their way around him. Luckily the metal was thick enough to stop them getting through. The gunfire ceased, and over the ringing in his ears Danny could hear Yuri going ballistic on the other side.

'Kill him, kill them all. Adrik come with me, we go to meet Knight and kill him.'

'Move back now,' shouted Danny to May and Ana as a guard charged out of the production room behind them, his gun swinging wildly. Already lined up, Danny squeezed off two rounds through the small gap between May and Ana's heads. The displacement of air moved their hair as the bullets passed. On their way they struck the guard's head dead centre, ripping the back off in a plume of red mist. Danny was moving before he hit the ground. He swung his head for a quick look into the room. Spotting the other guard staring at him down the barrel of an AK-47, he swung back out just as fast. The room exploded into deafening automatic fire. He could hear the sickening screams of workers cut down in the fire. Breathing slow he kept calm and waited, vibrations drumming in his back as bullets buried themselves into the brickwork on the other side. He heard a click as the magazine emptied and the shooting stopped. Dropping onto his side he tapped three shots through the doorway into the guard's centre mass, blowing him backwards as he frantically tried to load a new magazine into his AK-47.

'Quick, in here before they come through the door,' he said to Ana.

He could feel the phone in his pocket buzzing as Ana and May moved into the room behind him. Danny was pleased to see May looking more alert as she started coming out of her drug haze. Tucking into the doorway,

Danny took a knee and covered the metal door while he worked on a plan to get them out of there.

FIFTY FOUR

'Any answer from Danny?' said Bob to Harry as he placed the phone back on the hook.

'No, maybe the Russians got him, I don't know. We're out of time so I guess we go,' replied Harry, checking his handgun before putting it into a shoulder holster.

He slipped on his suit jacket and straightened his tie in the mirror.

I'm not going to let that Russian bastard think he's broken me.

He picked up a pump-action shotgun from the coffee table and walked past Bob towards the front door.

'We'll leave now, Bob. I've got to go somewhere first.'

Bob looked up but didn't question him. He'd been by Harry's side through good times and bad. Many enemies had challenged them over the decades, from the IRA to Jamaican Yardie gangs to the Kray twins. And now the Russians. Bob had come to terms with the fact they might not be coming back from this one. He looked down at the M16 assault rifle in his hand, took a deep breath and slowly turned, following Harry out to the car.

FIFTY FIVE

The metal door moved across a few inches. Danny loosened off a quick burst of automatic fire. In between the deafening return fire he heard the guards scampering back up the stairs.

I've gotta get on top of this, quick.

He stood to check on May, falling immediately back to his knee. His head was spinning again and the pain in his side was crippling. Taking deep breaths he made it to a table. May was much more lucid now and had a concerned look on her face, the destruction and bloodshed in the room behind her stressing Danny's need for action. Looking down, cocaine covered the table from bullet-ridden bags. Danny bent down and snorted a pile. An instant buzz flowed through his body, clearing his head and masking the pain in his side.

'Wait here until I come back. Anyone other than me comes down those stairs you shoot, ok?'

Ana nodded but May looked terrified.

'Don't leave us, Danny, please,' she said shaking.

Danny grabbed her arms and looked her straight in the eyes.

'You trust me, yeah? I'll be back in a bit,' he said. Still holding her he nodded his head. She eventually nodded back and he let go.

Loading his Uzi he gave it to Ana and took the Glock handgun back. Taking the silencers off both guns he checked and holstered one. Next, he took off his kit belt—he needed to move fast. Pulling out a flash-bang he moved to the metal door. Sliding through the open gap Danny moved near the stairs. He didn't get too close; he knew they would be waiting on the stairwell above him. Pulling the pin, he hurled the flash-bang up the stairs and tucked himself behind the wall, shutting his eyes and putting his fingers in his ears. The explosion of light and sound in the confined space was earth-shattering, blinding, and disorientating to the guards above. Danny was already on the move as the light died, a gun in each hand as he charged up the stairs. He took out two blinded guards as he ran up to the ground floor.

A burst of fire from somewhere further back peppered the wall above his head, showering him with plaster chips. Danny powered on up, shooting another of Volkov's men as he stumbled around. He emptied both clips across the factory towards the front door to keep their heads down. Instead of charging across towards them he hurtled up the stairs to the first floor, reloading the Glocks as he went. Ignoring the pain in his side and driven on by adrenaline and cocaine, he holstered one gun and ran full pelt across the floor. Grabbing the hose hanging from the roof, he jumped through the hole in the floor. The hose snapped tight before he hit the deck, swinging him across the ground floor in an arc. Danny targeted the two guards at the door, while they were still aiming at the stairs. He dropped one with two in the chest, then shot the other as he spun round in surprise.

His swing came to an abrupt halt when he crashed into a pile of old pallets. He lay there breathing heavily with both guns fixed in front of him for what seemed like an age. No one moved; no shots came his way. Eventually he dragged himself upright and limped towards the stairs. Remembering the phone buzzing in his pocket he took it out and had a look. Harry's home was on the missed call log. He called back, keen to tell Harry he'd got May back safe.

'Ello,' came Ron's gravelly voice.

'Ron, it's Danny. Can I speak to Harry?'

'No, he's gone with Bob to meet that Russian bastard for the exchange.'

'Shit, shit. I've got May. She's safe. Where did they go, Ron? We've got to stop them. Yuri's going to kill them both,' said Danny, his mind racing.

'Fuck, I don't know. Bob wouldn't tell us. He said he didn't want any of us following.'

'Ok, ok, fuck, I've gotta go,' Danny said, trying to think.

'Danny, wait. I overheard them say something about an airfield at two o'clock.'

'Ok, thanks.'

Danny rang off and made it back to May and Ana. When they got back up to the ground floor, he could hear the sound of sirens approaching in the distance. He turned to May and Ana.

'You'll be all right now, May, the police will be here in a minute. I've got to go and help your dad.'

May nodded, but Ana looked scared. This time it was May's turn to comfort her as Danny left. He ran back up the stairs leaping three or four at a time, all the way to the top floor.

As armed officers burst into the building through the big metal door, Danny's legs were disappearing out through the roof. He found his jacket and put it on, concealing his weapons once again. A few minutes later he walked calmly out of the reception and out onto the road behind a sea of police and flashing lights. As he made his way to the car, he glanced back at the factory. He could see May and Ana with foil blankets around them, being led to an ambulance. He lost sight as they passed behind a group of armed police. As they came back into view he smiled when he saw DCI Nichola Swan climb in the ambulance beside them.

FIFTY SIX

Bob sat back on the bench. The sun was shining through the tree-lined road that ran through the graveyard. The trees were full of young birds calling for their mums, all the noise and flapping filling the graveyard with contrasting life. He watched Harry in the distance as he placed flowers in the vase on his wife's grave. He contemplated the possibility that he, May and Harry could all end up here before the day was out.

It might have been nice to have a wife and kids, someone to remember him fondly, to grieve his passing, to carry his name.

He watched Harry moving through the rows of gravestones. He made his second visit to his sister Maureen's grave. He knelt down and carefully removed some dead flowers and leaves before replacing them with the second bouquet he'd brought with him. Bob could see Harry talking to Maureen; he didn't dwell on what he might be saying. Eventually Harry made his way back to Bob and sat beside him.

'You ready for this, Bob?'

'Ready as I'll ever be.'

'Well, we better get going then,' said Harry standing up.

Bob followed Harry out of the cemetery where the two friends walked side by side in silence, heading towards the car. They got in, still locked in their own thoughts before driving away to an unknown fate.

FIFTY SEVEN

Driving away from the factory, Danny's adrenaline levels dropped and his frustration and pain levels rose. Parking up a safe distance away, he sat in the car, gripping the steering wheel until his knuckles went white.

Think, think, how do I find out where they're going?

Only one idea came to mind. He had no choice other than to pursue it. Grabbing the phone, he called Scott.

'Daniel, old man. Where the hell have you been?'

'No time to explain, Scott. Time is of the essence so I need you to listen.'

'I'm all ears, old boy, fire away,' said Scott, intrigued.

'Have you still got the CCTV running from Silk & Lace?' he said lifting his shirt to see a yellowy red patch soaking through the bandages over his knife wound.

'Absolutely, it's better than the telly.'

'Is Dimitri there now?'

'He certainly is, he had a phone call about twenty minutes ago. Got him in a right flap; he's been packing stuff up and shredding documents. Looks like he's covering tracks or about to do a runner,' said Scott, pulling up the main camera in the office to take a closer look.

'Thanks, Scott, you're a bloody star,' he said, hanging up and starting the car before Scott had time to answer.

Yuri must have called Dimitri after seeing me at the factory.

He did a quick check for police vehicles and then hit the gas, pushing the speed as much as he dared in the capital's busy, narrow streets. He was only a few miles from Silk & Lace, but it still took a frustrating ten minutes to get there. With no parking bays close to the club, Danny left the car on double yellow lines and crossed to the entrance door. The club was closed and the door was locked. Danny banged on the glass continually until an angry-looking doorman with bulging muscles and no neck moved into the foyer.

'What you want?' he shouted through the glass in a thick Russian accent.

'Yuri sent me, I need to come in. I have a message for Dimitri,' said Danny doing his best to look annoyed and impatient.

'You wait there, I call up to him.'

'Look, if you don't let me in, Yuri's going to go fucking mental. Now stop pissing about and open the fucking door.'

The doorman stared at Danny, the cogs in his brain turning, looking for the right decision. He eventually moved to the door and pulled the sliding bolts at the top and bottom. The second he drew the door back Danny swiped him with a right hook on the side of the face. Apart from taking half a step back, the guy hardly moved. Danny's arm jarred on his chin like he'd just hit a brick wall.

The doorman's hand grabbed Danny's jacket and pulled him into the foyer with such force he crashed into the wall opposite. He would have shot the guy, but his jacket was still zipped up, and the doorman was coming at him fast. Danny dropped on his knee and punched him as hard as he could in the balls. Instead of dropping him, this just seemed to make the steroid-head angrier. He clamped two hands on Danny's throat and lifted him off the ground. Danny tried punching him in the side with no success. His head was spinning, and his eyes felt like they would pop out of his head. He powered punches into the doorman's face, still with no release.

With consciousness slipping away, Danny felt his leg bang into something hard. Reaching down, he grabbed the top of a fire extinguisher and lifted it off its mount. He clanged it off the side of the doorman's head with all his might. The blow knocked his head sharply over to one side, finally making him release his grip. Coughing and sucking in air in gulp-loads, Danny swung the extinguisher at the still-standing doorman. The blow caught him hard on the opposite temple. This time his whole body rocked to one side with the blow. Aggression unleashed, Danny drove the base of the metal extinguisher into the centre of the stunned doorman's face. The blow made him fall backwards in slow-motion, like a felled tree to the forest floor. Danny pounded him a few more times, just to make sure he wasn't going to get up any time soon. Standing upright he threw the extinguisher on the ground and peeled off his jacket. Pulling the Glock from its holster he pushed the inner foyer door open and moved inside.

FIFTY EIGHT

The light was dim inside the closed club. It was all quiet apart from the hum of the air-con and chiller fridges behind the bar. He moved along the front of it, with the stage on the other side. His focus was on the private door that led up to the office. He sensed someone coming out from behind the stage. A flicker in his peripheral vision gave him just enough time to twist and dive over the bar. As he landed on his back, one of Yuri's men sprayed the area with automatic fire. It ceased for a couple of seconds before ripping across the back of the bar, covering Danny in a cascading rain of liquor and glass. The second the burst of fire ceased Danny was up. He let loose two short bursts of fire in the direction he'd first seen the man. This guy was good—he'd moved into a defensive position between the seating booths. Danny just got his head back down before another volley of red-hot bullets screamed past him. They were so close to his head he could feel the heat of the bullets as they passed.

***

Frozen in his tracks, Dimitri stared at the CCTV monitor in the office. As if struck by lightning he dropped the paperwork in his hands and made for the phone.

'Yuri, he is here downstairs, shooting up the place,' said Dimitri in a nervous tumble of words.

'Stop whining, Dimitri. Who is there?' Yuri said, the annoyance clear in his voice.

'The fucking nephew, Danny Pearson, the one you fucking said your guys had trapped in the factory's basement.'

'Are you disrespecting me, Cousin? Viktor and I have taken all the risks for years while you sat on your arse getting very rich off the back of us. You're a Volkov, Dimitri. Fucking act like one and take care of it.'

Yuri hung up the phone without waiting for a reply, leaving Dimitri rushing for the desk. He pressed a little catch underneath it, releasing a secret compartment. Dimitri pulled out a pistol and magazine the police hadn't found. He fumbled nervously, sliding the magazine in as gunfire continued to echo downstairs.

***

Danny's gun clicked out of bullets as he worked his way to the kitchen door. He threw it down, pulling the other one from its holster.

'Mikhail, go in through the kitchen. We have him trapped,' shouted the guy pinning him down from the stage.

Shit, if I don't move, I'm dead.

Grabbing a large bottle of scotch, Danny smashed the top off and stuffed a dishcloth in it. Finding a lighter by a tub of cocktail sparklers he lit the cloth. Squeezing off a couple of rounds he forced the man's head down. At the same time, he stood with his arm already extended, targeting the guy tucked behind the seating booths. He launched the bottle, watching it fly in slow-motion. It dropped, smashing on the floor at the shooter's feet. The vaporising whiskey engulfed him in a ball of flame. His screams cut through the club as he stumbled a few paces before collapsing into the stage curtains.

By that time Danny was over the bar and bursting through the main kitchen doors. He hoped to surprise Mikhail as he went for the door to the bar. The plan didn't work. Mikhail opened up his AK-47 as Danny came in, forcing him to dive behind a stainless steel workstation. With his gun arm extending through the gap under the heavy steel catering unit, Danny shot Mikhail in the foot. A screaming stream of Russian profanities came from Mikhail as he fell back out of sight into a small alcove near the door to the bar. Using the advantage Danny moved back into the club. Smoke was building and a fire had taken a good hold up the stage curtains. Planting his back to the wall on one side of the private door, he used the back of his heel to bash the door open. A hail of bullets ripped through the open doorway, only stopping as the heavy fire door swung shut.

This is really starting to piss me off.

Holding his side, Danny gritted his teeth and ran through the smoke and hopped over the bar. Without breaking momentum he ran towards the kitchen door. Firing a line of shots through it from waist to head height, he kicked it hard, sending Mikhail's falling body flying. He trod on his back as he moved through, hearing a wheezy gurgling sound coming from the bullet holes in his chest. Spotting something as he made his way to the back door, he grabbed it and continued on his way. He was glad to see the courtyard was empty and stood for a minute, his hand resting on Viktor's red Ferrari. He started shivering uncontrollably before throwing up. The infection was much worse. If he didn't get to a hospital soon it could kill him. Shaking his head, he let his anger build until it took the place of pain. Tilting his head, he stared up at the office window, face hard, eyes burning and teeth gritted.

FIFTY NINE

'Did you get him, Pyotr?' shouted Dimitri to his man covering the stairs.

'I don't know. I think so, it's gone quiet.'

'Well, go and fucking find out, you idiot,' shouted Dimitri back to him, his face going red.

'Ok, ok,' said Pyotr as he moved down the stairs.

'And find out where that smoke's coming from.'

Dimitri backed into the office. He had the pistol in his shaky hand, covering the door as he moved. He stopped when he bumped into the corner of the desk, shivering a little from the breeze coming in through the open window. The thought suddenly crossed his mind: he hadn't opened the window. The barrel of Danny's gun pushed into the back of his neck.

'Where's Yuri meeting Harry?' asked Danny, reaching round to take the pistol out of Dimitri's hand.

'Fuck you, shithead,' said Dimitri, with Yuri's words, 'Y*ou're a Volkov, act like one,*' ringing in his ears.

'Put your hands flat on the desk,' said Danny, pushing the gun harder in the back of Dimitri's head.

Dimitri did as he was told with a sneer of defiance on his face.

'Right, we'll try that again. Where is Yuri meeting Harry?'

'Fuck you, you don't scare m—'

His words were cut short by the heavy chop of metal into wood. A few seconds later his brain caught up what his eyes were seeing. He pulled his hand to his body cradling it as he stared at the shiny meat cleaver stuck in the desk with three of his fingers sitting on the other side.

'That's for May. Last chance. Fuck me about again and I start hacking off bigger lumps. Where's Yuri meeting Harry?'

Danny moved in front of him, pushing his gun under his chin. He stared into Dimitri's shocked face, his eyes cold and vengeful.

'Yuri is meeting them at hangar seven, North Weald Airfield.'

'When?'

'At 2:00pm,' said Dimitri, his face white as a sheet as blood flowed down his arm and dripped off his elbow.

'Dimitri, where are you? We have to get out of here. NOW. The fire downstairs is out of control,' said Pyotr running back up the stairs.

He threw open the office door, stopping in his tracks at the sight of Danny. He tucked in behind the door frame, looking down the sights of his AK-47, trying to get a clear shot past Dimitri. Danny moved behind Dimitri. Grabbing the meat cleaver, he threw it smoothly at his target. It spun end over end, slicing a glinting path through the air. It ended in a sickening thud as it embedded itself in the centre of Pyotr's forehead. He went cross-eyed as he looked at it in disbelief. Slowly slumping forward, he stayed propped up against the door frame. Even though he was dead, his twitching nervous system locked his finger on the trigger. With the gun on fully-automatic, it emptied its magazine in seconds. Bullets ripped through and around the room, ricochets bouncing across in all directions.

When it was over, Danny had to check himself, amazed he'd not been hit. Dimitri, however, fell on his knees in front of him. Bullets had hit him in the chest and throat. His eyes looked at Danny wide with fear. Unable to speak, he fell to the floor, a thick, sticky pool of blood spreading out in front of him.

Danny moved to the window to see a cavalcade of police cars, fire engines and ambulances turning up out the front. He ran to the back window, pleased to see no one in the courtyard, just the red Ferrari parked below. Thinking quickly, he went through Dimitri's pockets and found the car keys. Making his way out the window he jumped down the fire escape a flight at a time. Wasting no time, he fired up the Ferrari and exited out from the archway, just behind the emergency vehicles. He drove away watching the police and firemen dragging hoses into the club in his rear-view mirror.

SIXTY

Turning the black Mercedes into the small, private airfield, Adrik drove through the raised barrier and past the security guard. The guard gave them a customary glance over the top of his newspaper, following them with his eyes to see where they went. Curiosity satisfied, he flicked his paper back up and leaned back in his seat in the security hut. Adrik continued past an empty office building built in World War II that was now only used for the occasional training course. He carried on past rows of small parked aircraft towards the larger hangars. They pulled up behind a small executive jet by the half-open door of hangar seven.

***

Sergei Poltz had been watching them from the minute

they entered the airfield. The ex-Special Forces soldier looked relaxed with his hands held behind him. He'd tucked them under his jacket, gripping onto the butts of two Glock 17's, holstered back-to-back just above his belt. Behind him stood the reluctant Trevor Bailey and Lenard Timms. Adrik had tracked them down after Dimitri's arrest. He told them they had one chance to redeem themselves, or he'd kill their families slowly as they watched, then kill them. Smiling, Adrik walked up and embraced his old colleague.

'Sergei, it's good to see you, brother,' said Adrik, his face dropping into a terrifying snarl as he approached Trevor and Lenard. He would have killed them, but Danny Pearson was causing him a serious manpower problem, so he needed them.

Stepping out of the car, Yuri didn't acknowledge them. He grabbed a large holdall out of the boot and walked past the hangar to the nearby executive jet. Banging on the side, he waited a second for the door to open. It folded down into steps and the pilot beckoned him inside.

'You ok, Yuri? I was just about to leave for the pickup in Amsterdam when you called.'

'Nothing for you to worry about. Open it up for me,' said Yuri, dismissing the question.

The pilot pressed the call buttons in a certain sequence and a plush leather passenger seat lifted to the sound of servomotors and slid back. It exposed a deep hidden storage hole. Yuri used several planes like this to bring drugs into small airfields. He unzipped the holdall and did a quick check of the used fifty-pound notes that filled its interior. Zipping it back up he stowed it in the hole and shut it back up again.

'Prepare the plane, Eli, I have to take care of something in half an hour. Then Adrik, Sergei and I will need to go to the airfield in the Ukraine. I have transport waiting there to take us to Russia.'

'Ok, no problem. I'm already fuelled up and ready to go.'

'Good,' said Yuri exiting the plane.

He turned on the bottom step and looked back at Eli.

'Whatever happens, whatever you hear, be ready to leave, you understand, Eli?'

Eli nodded before disappearing into the cockpit to do his pre-flight checks.

***

Adrik was telling Trevor and Lenard what to do as Yuri came in.

'Are we all set?' said Yuri to Adrik.

'Yes, I'm going to set up now,' said Adrik moving to the car.

'You two fuck-ups know what to do?' asked Yuri staring coldly at Trevor and Lenard.

They nodded nervously as Trevor repeated his instructions back to Yuri.

'Just stand back with our guns on show, If the shit hits the fan, come out shooting.'

'Good, now fuck off over there by that aircraft. Adrik will have them covered from the office buildings with the sniper rifle, and Sergei and I will take care of them from here.'

With Trevor and Lenard out of earshot, Yuri spoke quietly to Sergei.

'When this is over, kill those two idiots.'

Sergei didn't respond, the message was understood; an order was an order and he would carry it out without a second thought. They watched through the open hangar door as Adrik drove the black Mercedes across the tarmac. He disappeared out of sight around the back of the old office building where he parked the car. A few minutes later, they could just make out his hand pushing a window open through the vertical blinds on the first floor. Yuri's phone ringing caused Trevor to jump, the tension almost giving him a heart attack.

'Yes? Good.'

Yuri put the phone back in his pocket.

'Adrik is ready. Now we wait. They will be here soon.'

SIXTY ONE

'Fucking traffic, look at this lot,' said Harry sitting in the passenger seat while Bob drove.

'West Ham's playing at home today, kick-off's in an hour. Don't worry, Boss we'll be through it soon.'

'Lou used to moan about the traffic when West Ham played, reckoned she couldn't get parked anywhere near the beauty salon.'

Harry turned his head away from Bob to wipe a tear from his eye.

'I swear to god, Bob, if May's dead I'm gonna kill all those fuckers if it's the last thing I do.'

'If it comes to that, I'll be right there next to you,' said Bob grimly.

***

A mile behind them, Danny thudded the steering wheel with the palm of his hand.

Come on! Fucking traffic.

Seeing a gap, he dropped a gear and screamed up a bus lane as angry football fans honked their horns at him. A speed camera flashed him as he cut back into traffic ahead of the holdup. He checked the sat nav. Twenty-five minutes to destination.

At legal speed limit, once I hit the M11 I'll make up some time.

Another five excruciatingly slow minutes later, Danny finally hit the dual carriageway leading onto the motorway. Hammering the gears and screaming the revs, the Ferrari took off in the fast lane. Driving like a lunatic Danny weaved in and out of traffic at frightening speeds.

***

'Look at that fucking idiot,' said Harry as a red Ferrari crossed four lanes in front of him. It roared across from the outside lane and undertook two lorries on the breakdown lane. It reappeared ahead of them, weaving dangerously back into the outside lane again. With a scream of the exhaust, it accelerated away as if they were standing still.

'Christ knows how fast he's going. We're doing eighty.'

'Talking of speed, we going to be there on time, Bob?'

'Yeah, it's not too far now.'

SIXTY TWO

Taking the slip road off the motorway at Harlow, Danny followed the signs for North Weald Airfield. As he flew down the country lane, beads of sweat ran down his forehead and his vision blurred. He put the window down, hoping the blast of fresh air would clear his head. After several big breaths, his focus sharpened, and the airfield gatehouse came into view. Turning in, Danny noticed the overweight security guard sitting bored inside his wooden hut. He stopped and leaned out the open window.

'All right, mate, I'm supposed to be meeting some guys over at hangar seven. Don't suppose you've seen them, have you?'

The guard eyed him with disinterest over the top of his newspaper.

'Don't know, *mate*. I can't remember seeing anyone,' said the guard leaning back in his chair and raising his paper to block Danny from view.

Reaching into his pocket Danny peeled off a couple of hundred from his money roll.

'You absolutely sure about that?'

The paper lowered just enough for his eyes to come into view; they widened at the sight of cash and the paper lowered.

'Now you mention it, I did see some guys coming through on their way to seven. Three guys got dropped off two hours ago, a mean looking guy, shaved head, military type, you know. The other two looked shit-scared of him. They're still over there now. A little later two guys in a Merc arrived and drove over to the hangar. Ten minutes later the big guy with the blind eye and the scars drives back and parks by the office building over there.'

The guard pointed at an old building. Danny followed his finger to see the parked Mercedes.

'Odd thing, he went in with a long black case and never came out.'

Danny reached in his pocket again and added a couple more fifties to the pile and handed them to the guard.

'Thanks, buddy. You might want to make yourself scarce, ok?'

He didn't take much convincing, just folded his paper and left the hut muttering to himself.

'Bloody minimum wage, I don't get paid enough to deal with this shit.'

Danny pulled into the airfield deliberately taking a left, in the opposite direction to the hangar. He looped around behind some light aircraft, eventually parking out of sight on the opposite side of the building to the Mercedes. Walking cautiously along its rear, he soon found a door with a forced lock. Approaching with stealth had been a practiced skill in the SAS; it was one Danny had been very good at. But with blood poisoning setting in from the infection, he felt like he was crashing up the stairs in hob-nailed boots.

Sweat poured off his forehead as he slid up beside the door to one of the training rooms. Moving across just enough to see through the glass, he spotted Adrik sitting bent forward over a desk, his good eye glued to the sight of a high-velocity sniper rifle. Its legs were steadied on the desk and the barrel poked out through the vertical blinds. moved back, glad the element of surprise was still in his favour. He checked his gun.

Only two bullets left, shit.

He couldn't use them anyway; Yuri would know he was there and kill Harry and Bob on the spot. Instead, he holstered the gun and drew his serrated commando knife. Taking a few deep breaths to steady himself, he turned to the door just as it unexpectedly wrenched open. A large hand locked on his wrist while the other locked on his throat. Before Danny could kick him in the balls or headbutt him, Adrik lifted him clean off the ground and threw him like a ragdoll across the room. He crashed through the lined-up desks and chairs, dropping his knife as he went. Focusing his anger and adrenaline, he blanked out the pain and sprung to his feet. Adopting a fighting stance, he readied himself for Adrik's attack. He came at him fast, unleashing combinations of blows, kicks, and blocks. Both men adopted the Krav Maga style of hand-to-hand combat widely used by Special Forces around the world.

Danny knew it well. He blocked jabs and kicks, countering with the same in a brutal stalemate. Adrik's attack was relentless, forcing Danny slowly back towards the wall. Realising he was getting cornered, Danny leaped back and used the wall to launch himself forward. He swung in on Adrik's blind side with a powerful flying blow to the head. Adrik clattered sideways through the chairs, tripping and thudding loudly into a window, ripping the blind down on top of him as he went. Danny rushed in for the kill while Adrik was off balance. His concentration broke mid-step at the sight of Harry's car passing the exposed window. When his eyes moved back, Adrik grabbed him with both hands on one shoulder. In one swift movement, he pulled his knee into Danny's side with his full body weight and power behind it.

The blow was like being hit by a train. Danny crumpled, feeling the knife wound rip open. Grabbing the hair on the back of Danny's head, Adrik pulled his face up and headbutted him. The blow sent him sliding across the desk behind him, disappearing to the floor on the other side.

SIXTY THREE

'Where's the bloody hangar, Bob?' asked Harry, his patience and nerves both at their end.

'Steady, Boss, I see it over there. Fucking Ruskie bastards in front of it.'

Yuri stood on one side of the open hangar. As they got closer, Sergei appeared on the other. He gestured with his AK-47 for them to drive inside.

'Here we go,' said Bob.

'About fucking time. Let's get this over with.'

***

Throwing the table out of the way Adrik grinned at Danny sprawled on the floor, his scarred face bearing down on him like a character out of a horror film. Trying to clear his double-vision from the headbutt,

Danny tensed every muscle as he prepared for the incoming attack. Adrik stepped in to kick Danny in the face. As his boot came down Danny caught it between his hands. From his lying position he used his heel and stamped on the side of Adrik's knee. The cartilage gave way and he went down in a scream of agony. Danny hauled himself up, his hand slipping on the table from the blood from his opened wound.

***

Bob pulled up inside the hangar by two light aircraft. Sergei, Trevor and Lenard were spread around the hangar, their guns firmly fixed on them. Yuri stood back without expression, waiting for them to get out. Harry was out first, his short, stocky frame tense as he glared at Yuri defiantly. Bob got out the other side, slow, confident, maintaining the persona that the surrounding people were nothing.

'Where's my daughter, you fucking tosser?'

'In good time. You have my money?' said Yuri with a hint of smugness at being in control of the situation.

'Get the boot, Bob.'

He moved to the boot and popped the catch.

'Whoa, whoa, whoa, easy there, big man,' said Sergei, nudging Bob back with the nozzle of his gun.

He opened the boot and pulled out the shotgun, shaking his head. He threw it across the hangar floor to land under one of the light aircraft. Reaching back in Sergei pulled out a large holdall and walked over to

Yuri. He dropped it down and moved to his side, his AK-47 never leaving Harry or Bob as Yuri unzipped the bag. He took out a bundle of cash and flicked through it. Throwing it back in he zipped the bag back up.

'You got your money. Where's May?' said Harry with contempt.

***

Hopping up on his good leg, Adrik hobbled as fast as he could towards the sniper rifle. Danny went for his gun only to find it missing from its holster. He frantically looked around for it, spotting his commando knife instead. Kicking chairs out of the way as he went, he slid under a table and retrieved the knife. Turning, he ploughed his way back through the obstacles to get to Adrik before he reached the rifle. The two of them came together just as Adrik swung the rifle round to shoot. Danny grabbed the barrel. Holding it aside, he stepped in and punched the knife into Adrik's blind eye, piercing the brain as it slid in up to the hilt. They stood locked in position for a few seconds until the muscles in Adrik's body gave way and he slumped to the ground.

Breathing heavily, Danny laid the rifle back on the table and slumped in a chair. He put pressure on his side. Blood still seeped through his fingers and down his jeans. Fighting the dizziness and trying to still his shaking hands, Danny calmed himself and picked up the sniper rifle, aiming it through the open window.

***

Giving nothing away, Yuri pulled out his mobile and put it to his ear. His face creased as he glanced out at the office block waiting for an answer.

'Adrik, Mr Knight wants to see his daughter. Put him out of his misery.'

Yuri hung up without waiting for Adrik's reply. He stared at Harry, a small smile spreading across his face. A second later Sergei's head exploded, a fountain of red coating the nose of the plane behind him. Yuri's face froze in shocked surprise. Trevor and Lenard just looked at each other in panic. Bob didn't waste a second. He ducked under the plane and grabbed the shotgun. He pumped two rounds into Lenard's chest, dropping him on the spot. Harry pulled his handguns, but before he could get Yuri in his sights, Trevor, freaking out over Lenard's death, opened up his machine gun. His aim was wildly off allowing Harry to take cover with Bob behind a plane.

'What the fuck's going on? Where did Yuri go?' Harry shouted over the deafening noise of gunfire and ricocheting bullets.

'I think he went out the hangar door,' shouted Bob.

'We've gotta get rid of this prick or we'll lose him. He's the only one who knows where May is.'

***

After putting Adrik's phone down Danny slowed his breathing and concentrated on taking Sergei out. After he dropped him he watched as the chaos kicked off. He saw Harry and Bob take cover and Yuri slip out of the hangar, running towards the executive jet. Tracking him through the sight he tried to get him in the crosshairs as he went. His hands started to tremble as his focus blurred. He squeezed off a round and watched it miss Yuri's head, thudding into the hangar behind him.

Shit.

He tried to track him again, but he'd disappeared out of sight behind the jet. Abandoning the rifle Danny moved out of the room, half running and half falling down the stairs before stumbling out the door.

SIXTY FOUR

Letting rip with the pump-action shotgun, Bob kept
Trevor's head down behind a steel workbench. Harry
reached in behind the driver's seat and brought out the
M16 assault rifle. He stood up and locked eyes with
Trevor, who was pointing the machine gun straight at
him over the car roof. Harry froze, expecting to be
shredded with bullets any second. Instead, the red
Ferrari came screaming into the hangar and crashed into
the bench, crushing Trevor between it and the wall.
Smoke came off the tyres as Danny reversed to separate
its mangled front from the bench. Winding the window
down he shouted Harry's way.

'May's safe and sound. Now get the fuck out of here
before the police show.'

Harry and Bob looked at each other stunned as
Danny disappeared out the hangar door backwards in a

squealing cloud of white smoke. Danny screeched to a halt before snaking away as he jammed it in first and the tyres fought for grip.

They didn't need telling twice. Bob got in the driver's seat as Harry grabbed the bag of money by Sergei's headless corpse. The tyres squealed on the shiny concrete floor before they found grip, and Bob headed for the airfield exit. Harry looked towards the runway. He could see Danny in the distance, the Ferrari screaming its way after the jet as it taxied to the runway.

***

Redlining it in every gear, Danny fought with the steering to keep the car straight. The powerful engine growled into a scream behind him as he followed the jet onto the runway. Although the engine was fine, the crash in the hangar had damaged the steering and the car drifted from side to side erratically. A horrible noise came from the front and a strong smell of burning rubber indicated something was rubbing hard on a tyre. Continuing to push the car to its max, Danny got level with the plane just as it was powering up for take-off. For a few seconds he thought he would make it in front of the plane, forcing it to stop. He hit 160 and edged level with the cockpit, locking eyes with Yuri as he sat in the co-pilot's seat. As he inched forward the front tyre blew out, sending him spiralling off the runway. Luckily, the soft expanse of grass allowed the car to spin and spin around in clouds of turf and mud. He glimpsed Yuri's smiling face as the plane hit take-off speed and lifted into the distance.

'Fuck, fuck, fuck,' shouted Danny, punching the dash in a release of frustration. He pushed the door open and fell out onto the grass. The seat behind him shone slippery and wet with blood. He was vaguely aware of sirens in the distance as he tried to stand. His legs wouldn't hold him and he fell to his knees before moving onto all fours and vomiting violently. When he'd stopped, the world spun around him and he collapsed. With his eyesight blurring into unconsciousness, he could just make out blue flashing lights dancing their approach before he passed out.

SIXTY FIVE

When he woke up harsh light hurt his eyes. Danny instinctively tried to sit up, regretting the decision as pain ripped up from his side. As his focus sharpened, he found himself looking at a police officer sitting on a chair by the door. He tried to lift his left arm, only to find it held back by shiny handcuffs locking him to the bedrails. The officer rose without looking at him and stuck his head out the door.

'Ma'am, he's awake.'

Seconds later, DCI Nichola Swan entered the room.

'Could you give us a minute please, George.'

'Err, yes, ma'am. I'll be in the corridor.'

She waited until he'd closed the door before speaking.

'Glad to see you back with us,' she said, a caring tone in her voice and a sadness in her face.

'I've been told I have an annoying habit of doing that. Are you ok?' he asked, his eyes searching for answers.

She moved over to the bed and put her hand in his. A tear welled up in her eyes.

'I don't know. I want to help but it's out of my hands. You destroyed half of London. They're still trying to work out what to charge you with first.'

'Hey, it's all right. I got May back, that's all that matters. She's safe, you're safe, all's good. I'll take what's coming,' said Danny squeezing her hand.

'If people knew about us and what I did to help you, I'd lose my job and my career would be over,' she said, pulling her hand away from his.

'It's ok, I understand. As far as anyone else is concerned, we never happened.'

'Thank you. I'm sorry, Danny,' said Nichola wiping her eyes.

'Is the girl that was with May at the factory ok? Her name is Ana.'

'Yes, she's being looked after. I think she's being sent back to her family in Romania.'

'Good. I need you to do me one last favour. For old times' sake. Can I borrow your phone?' he said, the cuffs rattling on the rail as he moved his arms. Nichola nodded, glancing at the door before handing it to him.

'Make it quick. I don't want George to come back and see you,' she said, checking the door again. Danny dialled a number which answered immediately.

'Paul, it's Danny. I haven't got much time to talk, mate. I'm sending someone round. Can you give her four of the items out of the black holdall for me?'

Paul simply said ok and hung up. If Danny didn't have time to talk, Paul wasn't going to waste it. Writing Paul's address in Nichola's phone he handed it back.

'If you go to this address Paul will give you something to give to Ana. Tell her to go home and look after her family.'

Nichola nodded as George opened the door.

'Goodbye, Danny,' she said with a sad smile and then she was gone.

He lay back and stared at the ceiling. Medication and exhaustion must have kicked back in. His eyes shut and he fell into a dreamless sleep.

SIXTY SIX

Danny woke up at the same time a whole day later. Wiping the blur and sleep out of his eyes he realised the handcuffs had gone. Looking up he noticed George had gone too. In his place sat a man in an immaculate pinstriped suit, his wavy blonde hair neatly cut into short back and sides. His ice-blue eyes focused on his trousers as he picked a bit of lint off. Danny recognised the type— government, secret service or intelligence; they all looked the same. An all-important smugness emanated from them, usually because the deck was heavily stacked in their favour. Danny's face hardened and his stare intensified as he waited for the conversation to start. He knew he would want something—they always did.

'Thought you were going to sleep forever, Daniel,' he said at last.

His voice was jovial and his accent was straight out of Oxford or Cambridge.

'Well, I've been a little busy lately,' said Danny with a frosty response.

'Yes, you have, a very busy boy indeed.'

'How about we cut the crap and you tell me who you are and what you want?' said Danny, his patience disappearing fast.

'Fair enough. You can call me Howard and I'm here to make you an offer.'

'Howard what?' continued Danny aggressively.

'Take your pick, Smith, Jones... Now if you're quite done, I'll continue.'

Howard waited a few seconds and when no comment came he continued.

'At the moment you are facing a record-breaking list of charges: multiple murders, arson, possession of firearms, vehicle theft and a speeding ticket. You're probably looking at a hundred and fifty years in prison,' said Howard, pausing for effect. When he got no reaction, he continued.

'We've been following your career for quite some time. I particularly liked your unauthorised rescue of Mr Greenwood from Al Qaeda fighters in Afghanistan. Anyway, I digress. Your removal of the Volkov family from London has, how shall I put it, pleased some very important people. So much so that they have given me the green light to offer you a deal.'

Danny wasn't sure he liked where this was going. The revelation that this man had stopped him getting court-martialled for rescuing Paul against direct orders told him he had the power to make things happen. But at what cost?

'I can make all this go away. You can go home, carry on with your daily life. You can even keep the money you got from Volkov's safe.'

'Cut the crap, Howard, what is it you want in return?' said Danny, tired and impatient with the games.

'A man with your particular skill set is hard to find. From time to time we may ask you to do something for us. You will, of course, be paid very well for your services and discretion,' said Howard, never letting his friendly demeanour drop.

'And if I say no?'

'Entirely your choice, old boy. Get on with your life or get used to prison food.'

The room stayed quiet for several minutes while Danny brooded. He knew he had no choice but he didn't want this guy to take him for an easy sell.

'Ok, but I'm in charge, I do things my way.'

'Absolutely, I wouldn't have it any other way,' said Howard smiling.

He got up and made for the door, talking over his shoulder as he went.

'Get well soon, Mr Pearson.'

SIXTY SEVEN

Before Danny had time to dwell on Howard's visit, the door flew open and May piled into the room, her bright, smiling face lighting up the place and lifting his mood.

'Hello, Titch, how are you?' said Danny, her positive energy causing him to smile.

She ran over and put her bandaged hands around him, squeezing him tight. She jumped back when he flinched and grunted in pain.

'Oh God, sorry, are you ok?'

'Yeah, yeah, just a bit tender that's all. It's nothing serious,' said Danny with a chuckle.

It was so good to see her happy and safe.

'Good. I wanted to come sooner but the police wouldn't let me in. Are you in trouble?' she asked as Harry entered the room behind her.

'Apparently not. Are you?' he said looking past May at Harry.

'I thought I was, but now I don't think I am. Me and Bob spent two days solid getting grilled by plod. They threw everything at us from forensics on-site to gunshot residue on our hands. We stuck to the no comment bollocks with our solicitor but it wasn't looking good. Then some toff in a suit turns up, all smiles and handshakes. He thanks us for our assistance and says we're free to go. No further questions.'

'Great, so all good then. How are your hands, May?' Danny said, changing the subject.

'The pain's not too bad now. I'm just happy to be alive, and I've got spares,' she said pulling a face as she pulled a comical double thumbs-up.

Danny laughed and winced with pain at the same time.

Harry moved around the bed close to Danny and spoke quietly in his ear.

'Seriously, son, I owe you everything for saving May. Anything I can do for you, just name it. Money, work, anything.'

'You don't know a good kitchen-fitter, do you? I owe Rob a new one,' said Danny smiling back at him.

As if on cue, Rob and Scott came jostling through the door like a couple of school kids.

'You still in bed, old man? Rather milking it a bit for a paper cut, don't you think?' said Scott, his floppy blond hair bouncing up and down as he laughed at his own joke.

'Shut up, you tart,' said Danny his spirits fully lifted.

'Is everything ok, bruv? Is all this over?' asked Rob looking concerned.

'Yes, Rob, it's all over. I'll be out of here and home in a day or two. How's Tina after what happened at the house?'

'She's still a bit shaken up. The trashed kitchen keeps reminding her of dead Russian bodies. But apart from that she's peachy.'

'Ok, ok, I can take a hint. As soon as I get out of here I'll sort the kitchen out,' said Danny, happy to put the worries and questions to one side.

'If the serious chat is over I've got a little something for you,' said Scott with an air of mystery as he put two carrier bags on the bed.

Delving in he pulled out a McDonald's bag with burgers and fries in, then reached in the other bag and pulled out a six-pack of beer and handed them round.

'Scotty boy, you're a lifesaver, I'm bloody starving, mate,' Danny said cracking the can and raising it in a toast. 'To Mum and Lou,' he said, looking at his brother then Harry.

They raised their cans back and repeated the toast.

The afternoon went fast as they chatted and joked. Eventually a nurse came in and after frowning at the empty cans and food wrappers, told them Danny needed rest and they should leave. May kissed him goodbye and Harry shook his hand. Scott and Rob just waved and sniggered behind the nurse's back, leaving the room like they entered it—like naughty school kids. He couldn't

help but laugh, instantly regretting it as he winced in
pain.

SIXTY EIGHT

Looking up at the sun flickering through the thick, leafy canopy, Danny walked down the tree-lined drive of the City of London Cemetery. Sarah had always loved this time of year. That's when they'd got married. He turned at the grave with its ornate stone cross that he knew so well and headed down the long row of graves. When he reached his destination, he turned and went down on one knee. Taking the old flowers out of the vase he replaced them with a fresh bunch of tiger lilies.

'Happy anniversary, love. I came close to joining you this time,' he said in a whisper.

He read the headstone as he always did, the fear of forgetting worse than the pain of remembering.

Sarah Ann Pearson. Beloved Wife and Mother. I'll Love You Forever.

Turning to the smaller grave next to his wife's, he put his hand on top of the headstone.

'Hiya, son. Miss you, boy.'

He read the headstone as he had for his wife, taking it in as he always did.

Timothy Robert Pearson. Beloved Son. I'll Never Forget.

With a sadness in his heart he left, stopping on his way out at his mother's grave and then his aunt's. When he left the cemetery, he walked the short distance to the Tube station and made his way to Islington. Noticing the shiny new Greenwood Security sign above the door, he climbed the stairs. The office at the top was now organised, tidy, and a picture of efficiency. Trisha got up from behind her desk and greeted him with a warm smile.

'Hi, Danny, you look well.'

'Yeah, I'm almost as good as new,' he said, trying not to stare at her figure as she walked ahead of him to Paul's office.

'Danny, great, come on in. You want a tea, coffee?' he said getting up and making for the kitchen.

'Go and sit down. I'll do it,' said Trisha, disappearing out the door.

'You look a lot better. Sorry I didn't come and see you in hospital. I had to visit the seminar venues, risk assessments, security weaknesses, that kind of boring stuff. I only got back from Minsk Tuesday.'

'Hey, don't worry about it. I've had plenty of visitors. Scott even got thrown out for bringing me a crate of beer,' he said chuckling as he took a coffee off Trisha.

'Are you still up for the seminar gig? I can get someone else if you're not,' said Paul, concerned.

'Don't you dare, I'm fine. I just want to get to work and put the last few weeks behind me.'

'Good man, glad to hear it.'

They spent a while going through the details of the job and chatting. When Danny was ready to leave Paul unlocked a cupboard and grabbed Danny's holdall. He threw it on the floor by Danny's chair and sat down again.

'About time you put that somewhere safe, like a bank perhaps.'

'Err, yes, I suppose so. That actually brings me to another question I've been meaning to ask you,' said Danny, noticing Paul lean back with a knowing smile.

'You want to know who Howard is and who he works for.'

Paul always had an annoying habit of knowing what people wanted before they said it.

'Yes, I do,' he said back.

'Howard's one of the good guys, trust me. He's in charge of a very special division of national security. No official titles and very off the books.'

'Mm, and now I'm in his debt,' said Danny frowning.

'That's a maybe, but you were going to go after Yuri regardless of Howard. Without him you wouldn't have had the kit bag or the location of the factory and would probably have got yourself killed. If, by some miracle, you survived, you'd be sitting in a jail cell, and it was

Howard who stepped in when you saved me in Afghanistan, and got your charges dropped.'

'Yeah I know. Don't expect me to kiss his arse though.'

'What, and change a habit of a lifetime? Nah,' said Paul, lightening the mood.

'Ok, enough said, I've got to go. I promised Rob I'd buy a new kitchen before I fly out. I broke the last one with some bloke's head,' Danny said with a grin.

SIXTY NINE

The flight to Minsk went well. Danny sat with the security detail in economy, while the delegates flew up front in business class. He was fine with that. The guys he was working with were all ex-military and they fell back into barracks humour in the blink of an eye. He felt pretty good. The infection had all gone, and apart from the odd twinge his injuries had all healed up. The minibuses waited for them outside the airport as arranged, and within an hour they pulled up at the Victoria Olimp Hotel. It was the venue for the seminar and where they'd be staying before flying on to Moscow for the next round of talks.

The rooms were nice and the job was easy. The security at the hotel was overkill. Each country's delegates had their own security details, which accounted for half of the hotel's guests. The day's events had finished and the delegates were all safe in their hotel rooms or at the hotel bar. Danny walked through the foyer on the way back to his room. He shied away from the lift and took the stairs as usual. He walked down the plush carpeted hall to his room, tapping the key card on the lock. He entered and closed the door behind him. He was just about to put the card in the slot to turn the lights on when the hairs on the back of his neck stood up and a cold shiver ran down his spine. Something was off. He stood there in the dark, still and quiet, his hand frozen above the card slot. He forced his breathing down, slow, listening, while his eyes became accustomed to the dark. There it was, the other man breathing, barely detectable—more sensed than heard. The suite was large, split in two with a lounge and bedroom with an en-suite bathroom.

Where is he? Where would I be? Just inside the bedroom.

His eyes adjusted enough to see the room in an orange-silhouetted gloom from the street lamps outside. Moving in silence he grabbed the coat stand with both hands and lifted it, taking care not to tap it on the wall. He stood two feet short of the bedroom. His senses were in tune with the sounds of the room now, he could hear him breathing from within. Suppressing his nerves he waited to attack, sizing up the dimensions of the opening into the bedroom. Gripping the coat stand like a mace he placed his feet apart and silently counted in his swing, moving from side to side like a baseball batter.

One, two, three.

Without holding back he powered the coat stand around the door frame, while stepping through behind it. The hooked end found its target, knocking the shadowy figure clean off his feet as it broke into pieces. Danny heard the distinctive heavy thud of a gun being dropped.

He jumped at the moving outline on the floor, the broken stand raised above his head like he was about to stake a vampire. But his attacker was quick. He rolled to one side, leaving Danny to thump the point into the carpet.

A leg came back at him at lightning speed, the boot connecting heavily with the side of his head, knocking him sideways into the wall. Using it to spring back Danny got his elbows in and fists up. His attacker was already up, powering kicks and punches at him. Absorbing them, Danny moved inside the kicks and adopted the style of a Thai boxer, hammering a knee into the man's side. He followed by driving his folded arm up making contact under the chin with his elbow.

Danny tracked the man in the dark as he fell back from the blow. The man turned the fall into a backward roll over the bed and flipped upright, standing solidly on the other side. Danny caught the glint of a knife being drawn from its sheath.

Standing feet apart, knees bent, ready to move, he flicked his eyes from the man to the floor and back again. He did it again, still trying to locate the fallen gun, but the floor was too dark see it. As if sensing what he was doing, the attacker moved in, arms up, body weight spread, movements measured and trained. Danny moved to the end of the bed, keeping light on his feet, ready. He touched the broken coat stand with his foot and instinctively crouched, grabbing it with one hand. With the other hand he grabbed the bed runner and spun it around his forearm for protection. He barely had time to stand up before the man was on him. Danny felt the thud of the knife on his padded forearm as he went low with the stand, connecting solidly with the side of the guy's knee joint. As he went down Danny powered his knee up into the face. The nose broke and the man crashed to the floor on his back. Without waiting for him to recover, Danny spun the sharp end of the stand around and drove it up under the man's sternum into his heart. Danny watched him drop the knife and grab the pole sticking out of his chest with both hands. The shadowy figure moved slower and slower as his strength left him, his perforated heart bleeding out internally. He shook and convulsed, eyes wide in the orange light.

'Who sent you?' asked Danny kneeling on his chest and twisting the stand.

'Arggh, fuck you,' he said, blood bubbling out of his mouth.

'Who fucking sent you?' shouted Danny in his face, rotating the stick as the guy screamed.

'No, no, fuck. Yuri. Yuri Volk—,' he said, dying before he got the last word out.

Danny sat heavily down on the bed, breathing deeply. A few moments later he walked through to the lounge and put the card in the slot. Blinking at the harsh intrusion of light, he returned to search his assailant. Unsurprisingly there was no ID on him. It was obvious he was a professional paid to kill him. After a quick check of the empty corridor, he made a call.

'Paul, I need to talk to Howard. Urgently.'

'Stay by your phone,' said Paul hanging up, the tone of Danny's voice prompting him into action.

Within fifteen minutes, his phone rang with no number displayed.

'Mr Pearson, for what do I owe the pleasure?' said Howard, his tone polite and pleasant as always.

'I've got a dead hitman lying on my hotel room floor, courtesy of Yuri Volkov.'

'My, my, we can't have that can we? Are you hurt?'

'No, I'm fine,' said Danny calming down, his adrenaline levels dropping.

'Good, go down to the bar and get yourself a stiff drink. Be a good chap and give it a couple of hours before you return. I'll be in contact soon.'

The phone clicked off abruptly, leaving Danny alone in the quiet room. He changed his blood-stained clothes and went down to the hotel bar. A few whiskeys later he watched the clock tick over to 2:00am. Taking the stairs Danny made his way back to the room. He opened the door cautiously before entering. It was dark again. He put the card in for the light.

The room was immaculately reset, with a new coat stand in the corner. He moved through to the bedroom. The body had gone, and apart from a slight dampness where the carpet had been cleaned there was no trace.

They had tidied the room and laundered his clothes, leaving them neatly folded on the freshly made bed.

Tired and a little fuzzy from the whiskey, Danny undressed and climbed into bed. From his time in the SAS he followed a golden rule: take your sleep when you can. His head hit the pillow and he was asleep in minutes.

SEVENTY

Danny woke, his sleepy brain battling between the tidy room and the memory of last night's struggle. If it wasn't for the fresh bruises he might even have convinced himself it never happened. After looking at his old G-Shock watch he leaped out of bed.

Gotta get a move on, the flight to Moscow is in a few hours.

Showered, dressed and breakfasted, he downed plenty of coffee and boarded the flight to Moscow. Leaving the delegates in business class, Danny and his colleagues sat in economy. He wasn't in the mood for the usual small talk so he shut his eyes and slept for most of the flight. On arrival at the Crowne Plaza Hotel, he made an excuse at the check-in desk and got the receptionist to change his booked room for another. Avoiding the lift, Danny lugged his suitcase up four flights of stairs and down the corridor. As he stepped into his room, a figure sitting in the chair on the other side kicked his defensive instincts into action. He wrenched the suitcase up, tensing every muscle to launch it at as hard as he could in the stranger's direction. Just before release he realised who it was and eased the case to the floor, closing the door behind him.

'Changing the room at reception—a nice touch,' said Howard, sitting cross-legged and relaxed in the chair.

'Who was he?' said Danny bluntly.

'Ok, we'll dispense with the small talk. His name was Jaromir Klink, a very successful hitman—or I should say was—a very successful hitman. We've been after him for quite some time.'

'Is there anyone else after me? What about my family, Rob, Harry and May?' said Danny, more thinking out loud than asking the question.

'At the moment I don't think so. We found his rental car in a car park half a mile away from your hotel. From there we found his hotel and phone and cards, travel documents et cetera, et cetera. To cut a long story short, we found out he'd been paid half a million euros up front to kill you, with another half a million euros to be paid when the deed was done. At present, Yuri Volkov doesn't know he's failed or that he's dead. That puts the ball in our court, my friend. One I think we should take full advantage of,' said Howard, pausing to let the words sink in.

Danny wasn't slow on the uptake.

Take out Yuri before he finds out Jaromir is dead and hires the next hitman.

'And what did you have in mind?' he said, a little less hostile.

'So glad you asked, old boy. The Volkov family estate lies a twenty-minute drive west of Moscow.'

Howard pulled a large manila A4 envelope from inside his jacket and handed it to Danny.

'Plans of the estate, staff and security timetables and van keys. Exit the hotel past Costa Coffee onto Ulitsa Mantulinskaya street. There's a black Mercedes Vito van parked opposite. In the back you will find a package with some, how shall I put it, useful items in it. Be a good chap and park it in the same place with the keys in the glove box when you're finished. Oh, and wear some gloves,' said Howard getting up to leave.

He patted Danny on the back as he passed and paused at the door.

'It goes without saying, anything goes wrong, you're on your own. Good luck.'

Danny didn't answer or turn around. He heard the door click shut and turned his attention back to the contents of the envelope. He checked his watch. Just past midday. Throwing on a jacket, baseball cap and shades he left the room. After buying a street map and gloves from the nearest supermarket, he went to find the van. It was sitting where Howard said it would, and with a quick check both ways Danny slid the side door open. Two large canvas holdalls sat in the otherwise-empty van. He unzipped one for a quick look then zipped it back up and checked the second. He took out some powerful binoculars and threw them on the passenger seat, zipped the bag back up and slid the door shut. With the map open by the binoculars, he started the van and pulled off slowly into traffic.

He drove out of Moscow, keeping under the speed limit as he went. True to Howard's word, twenty minutes passed before he noticed the large, black iron gates of the Volkov estate. Without looking across or slowing down, he took in the two men on the gate and one wandering the grounds. A hundred metres further on he spotted the petrol station he'd circled on the map and pulled in. He parked in the far corner facing the mansion and out of view of the pumps and shop. He wandered across and bought himself a coffee and a sandwich so he wouldn't look out of place sitting in the van.

Danny alternated between studying the plans of the mansion and looking through the powerful binoculars. Just as the coffee was going cold a black Mercedes saloon pulled into the drive. A man appeared from the front, rushing to open the driver's door. Yuri Volkov stepped out. Ignoring his staff he straightened his suit jacket and walked into the house. Just seeing the man made Danny's body tense. Keeping his temper in check he swigged cold coffee before starting the van and turning out of the station. He drove past the estate again and on towards Moscow.

SEVENTY ONE

Danny spent the rest of the afternoon in his hotel room
running through the information from Howard. He
studied satellite images of the surrounding area from
Google Earth. Satisfied he knew the layout and security
backwards, he checked in with his team for tomorrow's
seminar arrangements. He feigned a dodgy belly when
they invited him to join them for dinner and drinks and
retired to his room. He got food from room service and
tried to get some sleep. He'd be leaving at one in the
morning.

***

Yuri tried the phone again; it went to voicemail again.

'Where the fuck are you? Call me. I want to know what's happening,' he said, calling Jaromir for the third time.

'Yuri, is he dead yet? What is the matter with you, eh? You are embarrassing the family. People are talking. They say we are weak.'

'Who says we are weak, Papa? Tell me. I will show them who's weak,' Yuri growled furiously.

'All the other families, that is who. They say you got your arse kicked by the English,' said the old man in a way only a father can do, to knock his son down a peg.

Yuri walked off while he could still hold his temper. If anyone other than his father had talked to him like that he would have killed them on the spot.

Where the fuck is Jaromir?

SEVENTY TWO

The alarm on his watch went off at midnight; it barely
got a beep off before Danny hit the button to silence it.
Dressed in black jeans and a black hoody pulled up over
a woolly hat, he left his room and took the stairs.
Avoiding bumping into any of his team he exited the
hotel, keeping his head down low. The van and its
contents were still in the parking bay where he left them.
After a quick look up and down the empty streets, he
started the van up and headed out of Moscow.

 As he approached the outskirts of the city, a police car
pulled out of a side street and fell in behind him. Danny
drove steadily on, trying to stop his heart pounding. In
the back of the van an array of weapons was laid out.
He'd stripped, checked, rebuilt and loaded them when
he returned earlier that afternoon. The seconds dragged
as he flicked his eyes between the road ahead and the

mirror behind. As if reading his mind, the lights spun on top of the police car as he stared at them in the mirror.

Shit.

With his mind racing, he ran through tactical options: try to out-drive them or stop and take them out before they called for back-up. The car pulled out and its sirens came on to join the lights. To Danny's relief it sped past him on its way to a call. He sighed and focused on the job in hand.

The next ten minutes dragged until he finally saw the Volkov family estate looming ahead of him. To his annoyance, the front was heavily floodlit. Turning right he took a single lane road that ran down the wall of the estate, and on between fields and farm buildings. He was glad to see the back of the building was not floodlit. In fact, there were no lights on apart from the odd room inside, and a wall lamp by the back entrance. With the Google Earth satellite images ingrained in his mind, Danny drove on a hundred metres from the rear of the perimeter wall. He turned in behind an old storage barn and killed the engine. He sat there for a minute or two, letting his eyes adjust to the dark and listening for any approaching cars or people on foot. When none came, he got out and slid the side door open. He'd already pulled the fuse for the internal lights and reached into darkness, picking up some night-sight goggles. Putting them on he surveyed the prepared kit in its green detail. After clipping, zipping and fixing the ammunition and weapon vest over a tactical jacket, Danny chambered a silenced Russian-made Kalashnikov handgun and holstered it. Lastly, he picked up a Kalashnikov SVK silenced assault rifle.

I guess Howard doesn't want an international incident if I get killed or caught. It wouldn't do to have British or American weapons on him.

He headed off at a fast tab across the field, tucking in tight behind the garden wall. Taking a minute to calm his breathing, Danny removed the night vision goggles and pulled himself up the eight-foot wall. He held himself steady, with his head peeping over the top as he scanned the back of the house. The light from the windows and wall light was too bright for night vision and would have whited the goggles out. A guard stood by the back of the house around forty metres away. Danny reckoned he was far enough away not to be heard and dark enough not to be seen. Pulling himself up, he swung his legs over and dropped into a crouch between the shrubs.

Taking a knee, he steadied the rifle and took a closer look at the guard through the powerful sight. The man was armed with an AK-47 and had a walkie talkie clipped to his belt. Breathing slowly he rotated left and right checking the back of the house. He couldn't see anyone else in the grounds or looking out the windows. He returned his sights back to the guard, exhaled slowly and squeezed the trigger.

The rifle made a small pop, and the guard dropped silently to the floor. Danny moved across the lawn fast and low. Grabbing the guard under the armpits he dragged him hurriedly back into the shrubbery. Slinging the rifle across his back, he pulled out his silenced handgun and made the return journey to the back door and entered. Sweeping the rooms of what would have been a servant's entrance, he turned into the kitchen and came face-to-face with one of Yuri's men tucking into a sandwich. Danny rammed his palm up into the man's face, pushing the sandwich into his mouth to keep him quiet. At the same time, he pushed the barrel of his silenced gun into the man's sternum and triggered two shots through his heart. He held his hand clamped across the man's mouth until the shocked look fell from his face and he dropped to the floor. Picking him up under the arms, Danny dragged him into a toilet off the corridor and shut the door. Using a knife, he twisted the slot on the outside to lock it behind him.

With the house still quiet, he moved into the empty dining room and crossed to see into the grand hall. A light was on in a room at the far end. As Danny moved closer he could hear a voice mumbling through the half-open door. With his gun's aim in perfect sync with his focus, he moved into the room. The sound came from an old man slouched in a chair behind an antique leather-topped desk. The old man's ice-blue eyes locked on Danny over the top of a half-empty vodka bottle. Neither of them moved. The old man's hands were hidden from view beneath the table.

'You are him—the Englishman. I knew you would come. You're going to kill Yuri, aren't you?' he said, his face soft but his voice hard and his eyes burning defiantly.

Danny paused, conflict ticking through his mind. Should he kill the old man or leave him? His mistake. The desktop exploded in a shower of splinters and shotgun pellets.

SEVENTY THREE

The noise woke Yuri up with a start. He pulled on a robe and headed for the door.

That bloody old shotgun. He is going to blow his own head off one of these days.

Hesitating, Yuri stopped before the door and backtracked. He slid the bedside drawer open and pulled out a stubby revolver. Putting it in his robe he hurried down the stairs, meeting the guard from outside as he ran in from the front.

'Is your father again?' he said as they headed for the study.

'Yes, Stefan, he's been drinking again,' replied Yuri, barely hiding his annoyance.

Entering the room first, Yuri saw his father through the smoke. He was sitting back in his chair with a large, smouldering, U-shaped hole blown through the top of the desk. As the smoke thinned, a bullet hole in the centre of his father's forehead came into view. Momentarily stunned, Yuri's focus was drawn to the spots of blood on the floor at his feet. He turned to face the barrel of Danny's gun.

Standing tight behind the door, Danny's eyes locked with Yuri's, leaving him in no doubt about his intent to kill. Blood dripped from his gun hand as it ran down from the peppered buckshot wound in his shoulder. Yuri's eyes widened as he watched Danny's trigger finger start to move. As it went through its final millimetre, Stefan shoulder-charged the other side of the door, crashing it painfully into Danny's wounded shoulder. It knocked him sideways, sending the bullet millimetres from Yuri's ear. His survival instinct kicking back in, Yuri pushed Danny's gun away and punched him in the injured shoulder as hard as he could.

Reeling, Danny saw Stefan coming in from the side, and lunged forward with his head slightly down, connecting it hard on Yuri's nose. The impact crushed it and put Yuri on his arse. Danny was bringing his gun hand around to deal with Stefan when the large Russian slammed Danny's hand into the wall, forcing him to drop the gun. The two men went straight into a fierce dance of blocks and powerful punches. Danny's injured shoulder and the rifle on his back were slowing him down. Stefan took full advantage of it. He moved fast, attacking Danny's injury at every opportunity. Left with no choice, Danny ducked and grabbed Stefan around the waist lifting him up and charging towards the desk.

He slammed Stefan down on the edge of the desk, impacting him hard in the small of his back. Moving away, Danny swung the rifle up from behind him, pulling the trigger just as Stefan got up. The round ripped through the centre of his chest, tearing his heart in two. Clutching at the wound he stared at Danny, his eyes wide. He coughed up blood as he attempted to speak. No words came out before he collapsed to his knees, toppling forward on to the floor.

Danny turned his attention to Yuri, who was frantically pulling at his pocket. He eventually ripped the revolver out of his robe and looked for his target. Danny was already ahead of him. He knelt on Yuri's chest, grabbing his wrist and gun with both hands. Staring into Yuri's eyes he slowly forced the gun towards his bloody face. Yuri's arms shook as he fought against Danny with every ounce of strength he had. For the first time, fear crept across his face as the barrel was pushed up under his chin.

'Fuck you,' Yuri spat in a last act of defiance.

'No, fuck you,' said Danny putting his finger on top of Yuri's and pulling the trigger, blowing the top of Yuri's head across the carpet.

Picking his silenced gun up, Danny raised it in front of him and worked his way carefully back the way he came. He paused in the kitchen to look around. After checking under the kitchen sink, he swung the rifle off his shoulder and smashed at the gas tap by the cooker repeatedly with the rifle butt until it broke. The hiss and smell of gas quickly filled the room. He grabbed a bowl from the cupboard and filled it with ammonia cleaner from under the sink. After dropping a metal dish scourer in he put it in the microwave, turning it on max. Grabbing a raincoat by the back door he checked the garden before running at full pelt for the wall. He'd just landed on the other side when the microwave blew, igniting the gas. The explosion shook the ground he stood on. Shards of blown-out glass tinkled off the wall behind him. He could faintly hear shouts from Yuri's men at the front gate. Paying them no notice he crossed the pitch-black field to the van. Sliding the side door open he eased his bloody vest and jacket over his injured shoulder. The blood had congealed around the shotgun pellets and wasn't dripping down his arm anymore. He dumped them and the guns in the back and gently pulled the raincoat on to hide the wound. Turning back onto the main road, he could see the guards out the front shouting down their phones in a state of helplessness while the centuries old Volkov family estate was being consumed by smoke and flames behind them.

That should keep the authorities busy until well after I've left the country.

He tucked in behind a fuel tanker and cruised slowly, invisible in the traffic as he entered the city. Several police cars and a fire engine sped past on the opposite side of the road, their lights spinning and sirens blaring as they rushed to the Volkov estate. By the time he parked the van back on Ulitsa Mantulinskaya street he had started to relax a little. He threw the keys in the glove box and walked up to the hotel. Just before he got there he peeled off the blood-covered latex gloves and tucked them in his pockets. Glancing back at the street some two hundred metres behind him, an empty space now sat where he'd parked the van. It was a chilling reminder that if things had gone wrong, he'd have disappeared without trace as fast as the van had. Putting his hood up and keeping his head down, he moved through the hotel lobby and up the stairs to his room. Stripping off, he put all his clothes in a carrier bag before painfully picking the shotgun pellets from his shoulder with tweezers. He flushed the shot and showered before dressing the wound and throwing on some clothes. Minutes later Danny walked a mile or so from the hotel. After checking no one was around he threw the carrier bag in a dumpster behind a convenience store. It was getting on for half-three by the time he collapsed into bed. Despite the shot and cuts and bruises, he was asleep within five minutes.

SEVENTY FOUR

Danny's pocket vibrated with the steady rhythm of an incoming call. He pulled out his phone and smiled.

'Hey, bruv. I'm just about to get a taxi to yours.'

'No, don't do that. I'm with Scott. We're pulling into the pickup bay now,' said Rob.

Danny was about to ask what they were driving when he was deafened by a loud exhaust and thumping music. Rob climbed out of an Audi RS6 and the two brothers hugged.

'Get a room, you tarts,' said Scott, turning the music down.

Same old, same old.

'What happened to the Porsche?' Danny asked Scott.

'The wife came back,' said Scott glumly.

'That's good isn't it?'

'No, old boy. She came back and took the Porsche and the house and pretty much everything in it. I'm staying at The Savoy.'

'Oh, sorry to hear that, Scotty,' said Danny, patting his friend on the shoulder.

'Yes, I know, it's a bloody shame. I loved that car.'

'You arsehole,' chuckled Danny.

Scott gunned the Audi out of the pickup zone and headed across London. Along the way Danny spotted a familiar graffitied wall, the red square with a yellow star above a yellow *V*. It had faded and weathered and now had *RIP* sprayed across it. Rob leaned forward from his seat in the back and spoke quietly in his ear.

'I went to Mum's will reading while you were away,' said Rob, followed by a long silence.

'The house is all paid for and she had just over twenty thousand in savings to be shared between the two of us.'

Danny sat very still for a long time. The emotional rollercoaster of the last few of months hit him in repressed waves, his wife and child, his aunt's murder and his mother's illness. He pulled himself back together, taking another minute before answering.

'The house is yours, Rob. You took care of Mum while I was away. You were there for her after Dad died. You deserve it, mate, and I won't take no for an answer.'

Rob was going to argue, but he knew his brother well. When he made his mind up about something there was no changing it.

'There is one condition, though,' Danny finally said.

'What? Anything.'

'I can stay until I've saved up enough money to buy a place. Unlike the love doctor here I can't afford to live at The Savoy,' he said with a wide grin.

'You're on,' said Rob as they pulled up at their mum's house.

'You coming in, Scott?'

'No, I'm taking the rather lovely little brunette from the hotel reception out for dinner tonight,' said Scott with a cheeky smile.

Danny just laughed as Scott dropped them off and left. They entered the house to be greeted by Tina in the hall. She gave Danny a hug and kiss before they went through to the kitchen.

'The new kitchen looks great,' said Danny, skimming his hand over the marble worktop.

'Yeah, they finished last week. I don't know how you afforded it. This must have cost a fortune.'

'Nah, it was an ex-display, got a fantastic deal on it. I'm just going to get changed,' said Danny, disappearing upstairs. He put his bags down and pulled some fresh clothes out of the wardrobe, the sight of the black canvas holdall tucked at the back making him smile. His phone buzzed with a message from Paul as he made his way downstairs:

'Good to have you back. Come and see me soon. I have more work for you.'

He entered the kitchen to find Harry and May had turned up with takeout and beer. Harry shoved a drink in his hand and with the people he cared about around him, Danny joined in with the laughter and chat.

It was good to be home.

Please, please, please leave a review for Vodka Over London Ice

As a self published indie author, I can't stress enough how important your Amazon reviews are to getting my work out there.

I love writing these books for you, it takes eight months of hard work to create each one. So please take a few minutes to follow the QR book link below, scroll down to reviews and leave a short review or just star rate it.

Thank you so much
Stephen Taylor

Please review Vodka and Jellied Eels

Choose your next Danny Pearson novel

The Danny Pearson books can be read in any order,
But here they are in the order they were written:

Vodka Over London Ice

The London mob clash with the Russian Mafia.
The death and violence escalate, putting Danny's family in danger.
Danny Pearson has to end the war, before more family die…

Execution of Faith

Terrorists and mercenary killers plot to change the balance of world
power. Can Danny Pearson stop them or will this be his downfall…

Who holds The Power

As a Secret organisation kills, corrupts and influences its way to
global domination. Danny Pearson must stop them and their deadly
Chinese assassin in his most dangerous adventure to date…

Alive Until I Die

When government cutbacks threaten project Dragonfly. General
Rufus McManus takes direct action to secure its future. Deep
undercover with his life on the line, can Danny survive long enough
to bring him to justice…

Sport of Kings

When Danny's old SAS buddy goes missing, Danny's unit reunite to
find him. When they follow Smudge's trail, they find themselves on
the wrong side of an international drug smuggling operation and the
sport of kings, an exclusive hunt of a deadly nature…

Blood Runs Deep

Five years ago (Vodka Over London Ice) The London mob clashed
with the Russian Mafia putting Danny's family in danger. Danny
Pearson ended the war, or so he thought…

Command to Kill

When Australian billionaire Theodore Blazer takes advantage of todays plugged in world with sinister intentions, Danny has to travel to the far side of the earth to save his friend Scott and stop the world falling apart…

Leave Nothing To Chance

When Danny's best friend Scott goes missing from his hotel room in Brazil, Danny pulls out all the stops to find him. The search takes him into the heart of Colombia and the clutches of a drugs baron known as El Diablo.

Won't Stay Dead

Snipe's back, awoken from his coma and with no recollection of the past few years. When the facility recondition him and put him to work, everything is fine until his memory and insanity return.

Till Death Do Us Part

Danny, his best friend Scott and his old SAS buddies travel to Benidorm for his stag weekend. After a boozy night out, they save two women from their hotel being hassled by some locals. But all is not as it seems.

Amazon Author Page

Available on Amazon

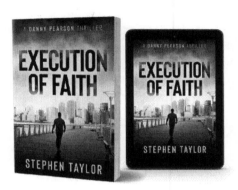

Read on for an extract from
EXECUTION OF FAITH

ONE

'Morning, Nigel. Where's the prince? Still in bed?' said Danny Pearson to his security colleague Nigel as he entered the penthouse suite of the Hyatt Regency in Dubai.

'No, no, he's having a swim up top. Says he's going to attend the plastic pollution seminar this morning,' Nigel replied.

Both men raised their eyebrows.

'Anything else.'

'Nah, oh, apart from we gotta new guy making up the rooms.'

The hairs on the back of Danny's neck stood up as he moved quickly into the master bedroom. Spying the abandoned cleaning trolley triggered images of the maid he'd passed in the corridor looking for her cleaning kit. From the top of the stairs he heard the faint click of the rooftop terrace door shutting.

'Nigel, on me. Cody, get your arse up to the terrace *now*,' shouted Danny through the radio, already halfway up the stairs.

Reaching the door he stopped, allowing himself a second to assess the situation. He hoped he'd got it wrong. The prince was climbing out of the far end of the pool, unaware of the young Arabic man in the hotel uniform walking towards him, a towel by his side, one corner held awkwardly.

Danny opened the door and slipped through, with Nigel behind him. He heard movement at the bottom of the stairs– Cody entering the apartment. Danny walked forward on his toes, silently. The man was unaware of their presence, his focus fixed firmly on the prince.

Cody burst through the terrace door like a bull in a china shop. Everyone froze, then looked at each other. The man's eyes went wide with fear before narrowing with determination. Dropping the towel, he exposed a three-foot curved Arabian sword glinting in the sun light.

The scene went from still to crazy in a blink of the eye. The man raised the sword and ran screaming in Arabic at the horrified prince. Danny powered after him trying to catch up. Not fast enough. There was only one course of action. As the attacker rounded the corner of the pool Danny used a sun lounger like a trampoline and launched himself into a dive, body-tackling the swordsman now just a few feet short of the prince.

They crashed into the sofas and coffee table. The small, lean swordsman swung wildly with the razor-sharp blade. Danny pulled one of the seat cushions in front of himself. The sword almost cut it in two, its silver tip only inches from his nose. He shot upright as the sword drew back, adrenaline pumping through his veins as if charged with electricity. Jumping back in time to avoid the swishes of a double swipe, Danny grabbed the corner of a towel off the seat beside him. He whipped it quickly at the glinting blade as it sliced its way towards him. The towel spun around the sword, catching tightly on itself. Using his power and weight advantage, he wrenched hard. The sword flew from the attacker's grip and plopped into the pool.

The swordsman stood stunned as Danny threw his full weight into a punch. The attacker's nose moved one way and his head the other. The blow sent the little man flying backwards over the sofa. Nigel and Cody dived to apprehend him. They needn't have bothered—he was flat on his back, out cold.

Shaking his bruised fist, Danny turned to check on the prince. He'd expected the man to look shocked and shaken but His Royal Pain in the Arse was grinning from ear to ear, jumping up and down and cheering.

Two days. Just two more days and I go home.

TWO

The neglected six-storey apartment building stood on one of the less desirable streets in Greenwich Village, New York. A rusted fire escape zigzagged down the front between windows peeling with old black paint. The communal entrance door was scratched and worn around the lock through which residents had stabbed their keys a million times over the years. On the wall to the left of the door were twenty-four buzzers. Most were covered with tape or labels on top of labels that hid an ever-changing history of occupants. In his one-bedroom apartment, Bradley White rifled through a pile of dirty washing until he found an old sweatshirt. It passed the sniff test—just. He'd worked night and day for the past two weeks and his domestic duties had been rather neglected. There were no clean clothes and the kitchen sink was besieged by a large, teetering pile of crusty cups, plates and cutlery. The whole lot stunk. Undeterred Bradley generously sprayed himself and the sweatshirt with deodorant, and pulled the garment over his head, onto his skinny torso through a cloudy aerosol haze. He checked his emails while brushing his greasy hair. His eyes lit up as a CMS payment email pinged into view.

'Shit! Oh, yes!'

He jumped up and hunted for his phone, eventually finding it wrapped up in his bunched duvet. Logging onto his banking app he waited. After a few tense seconds, $2135 displayed on the monitor.

'Yes!'

He thumped down on the beaten-up old sofa, bought from a garage sale around the corner. Letting out a big sigh, he gazed up at the damp patch in the corner. The mould was creeping its slimy way down from the ceiling to the wall.

Gotta get out of this shithole.

Leaping up he grabbed his keys and wallet, then slammed the door as he left the apartment.

It was a warm spring morning, and the short walk lifted his mood. He was starting to feel positive about his future prospects.

Bradley grabbed a seat outside his favourite coffee shop in the heart of the Village. This was the trendy part of town, he went there two or three times a week pretending it was because he liked it so much. In reality, it was because he fancied the waitress and was trying to work up enough courage to ask her out. Sitting nervously as she came over he only managed to stutter his order, failed again. He sipped his latte and munched on a frosted doughnut, taking peeks at the waitress from the corner of his eye as she served drinks and cleared tables.

The phone vibrated in his pocket. He took it out and looked at the caller ID. *Shit.*

'Err, hello?'

'Bradley, it's Marcus. I've just been going over your program submission. Excellent work. We are most pleased.'

'Okay, th-thank you,' said Bradley nervously.

'I trust you have upheld the confidentiality agreement,' said Marcus. His English was perfect, his tone devoid of emotion.

'Yeah, I mean of course. There's nothing other than the copy I sent you and the working copy on my computer,' said Bradley quickly.

311

'Excellent. I'll be in New York next week on business. We'll meet then and discuss your future with CMS. Oh, and pay your completion bonus, of course.'

'Yes, great. Thank you, Mr Tenby. I look for—'

Tenby had already hung up. Still, yes! At last, the break he'd been waiting for. Now he could move out of his shithole apartment and get something more in-keeping with his up-and-coming status. Yep, this was a great day.

Finishing his doughnut he picked up his coffee cup, then strolled off down a quiet side street with a spring in his step. He headed towards Fifth Avenue and Washington Square. Passing Kremer Property Lettings, Bradley paused to browse the window displays. Pictures of modern uptown apartments previously only dreamed of now leaped out at him. He continued walking, daydreaming of a posh new apartment, then turned his thoughts to lure of an immediate shopping spree.

As he crossed an intersection, someone called him. He paused halfway.

'Hey, Bradley, over here.'

Turning to look, his eyes searching the other side of the street for the source of the voice. It came from a service bay opposite. Large refuse bins lined up neatly along its rear. In a doorway to one side, a figure in blue workwear and a baseball cap waved at him.

'Sorry, do I know—'

His legs buckled from under him. The sound of bones breaking below the knee vibrated sickeningly through his body. Time froze in his mind's eye like a sports playback, delaying the massive impact on his lower back milliseconds later. His head and shoulders whipped back and struck a hard metallic surface, as it reverberated to his core. The delivery truck hit Bradley hard from behind. Its bumper shattered his legs before his lower back made contact with the curved front. He stared at the blue sky as his head and shoulders were forced backwards, planting him firmly onto of the sloping metal surface of the hood. With his head tilted upwards in a paralysed gaze, he was carried across the street into the service bay. As the truck collided with the bins, its metal sides bent around Bradley's body. He coughed a fountain of blood through his mouth as his internal organs were crushed.

In the seconds before consciousness left him and the life seeped out of his broken body, Bradley looked at his hand and blinked. It was settled, as if purposely, on top of the refuse bin, the coffee cup wedged upright.

This isn't right. My job, my money, my apartment...

BUY NOW ON AMAZON

About the Author

Stephen Taylor is a successful British Thriller writer. His Amazon bestselling Danny Pearson series has sold well over 150,000 copies, and delighted lovers of the action and adventure thriller genre. Before becoming a novelist, he ran his own business, installing audio visual equipment for homes and businesses.

With the big 50 approaching, Stephen wrote the book he'd always wanted to. That book was Execution Of Faith. A supercharged, action packed roller coaster of a ride that doesn't take itself too seriously. People loved the book so much he wrote a prequel Vodka Over London Ice. Because of the timeline, this became the first in the Danny Pearson Thriller Series.

Born out of his love of action thriller books, Lee Child's Jack Reacher, Vince Flynn's Mitch Rapp and Tom Wood's Victor. Not to mention his love of action movies, Die Hard, Daniel Craig's Bond and Guy Richie's Lock Stock or Snatch. The Danny Pearson series moves along with hard and fast action, no filler, and a healthy dose of humour to move it along.

Www.stephentaylorbooks.com

315

The Danny Pearson Thriller Series

Printed in Great Britain
by Amazon